LINDA HUGHES

THE PROMISE OF
Christmas
PRESENT
2
A MACKINAC ISLAND NOVELLA

THE PROMISE OF CHRISTMAS PRESENT

A MACKINAC ISLAND NOVELLA

LINDA HUGHES

For Violet, Valerie, Vivian, and Vance

CHAPTER 1

*C*hristmastime, 1837

Seven-year-old Cassie McIntyre managed to land a solid upper cut under the chin of her ten-year-old cousin Ian before her pa hauled her off him. "Liar, liar, lick spit!" she hollered as Pa dragged her away, arms and legs flailing.

When they were far enough apart from the crowd – gathered in the center of town for the raising of the Christmas tree – he swiped the snow off a tree stump and plopped her down on it. He had the look every child knows, the one that says, "I brought you into this life and I'll destroy your life if I want to."

No fool, despite her quick temper, Cassie shut up and sat still. She did, however, lean sideways ever-so-slightly to look around Pa, who stood in front of her with his hands on his hips like a stone giant. She could see that back at the scene of their scuffle, Ian, too proud to admit defeat, hustled to stand up, leaving behind a spray of blood, red dots on white snow, from the scape under his chin. He slapped snow off his heavy winter clothes and squared his scrawny shoulders. "I'm not a li..!" he yelped but his pa, Cassie's Uncle Niall, cut him off by grabbing the back of his collar and yanking him away in the opposite direction. Cassie couldn't see what her uncle said to his son, but her nemesis's face fell like that of a convicted man. She hoped his bum already stung from the whupping that no doubt would strike when they got home.

"Cassie," Pa quipped, his Irish accent more pronounced than usual, "look at me." She obeyed, doing her best to cast a sweet, innocent gaze at him. She hated it when he didn't call her Cassie Colleen like usual, her middle name being an Irish endearment meaning beautiful. This wasn't good. She bit her lower lip in dread. "You cannaw hit people. We've had this discussion once a'fore. What part o' that conversation did you naw understand?"

"Ah, well, um, but …" He referred to last year when she'd slugged Otis Redman in school for saying Ma was a savage. Ma was no such thing. Gichigama Geneviève St. Croix McIntyre had an Odawa mother and a French father and was married to an Irishman. She spoke four languages. Stupid Otis Redman could hardly speak one.

"Nae 'but.' There's nae hitting. If you have a problem, you come to Ma and me and tell us what 'tis."

"But, but you and Uncle Niall fight."

His voice relaxed. She'd hoped that, as usual, he'd soften for his only daughter, something he seldom did for her three younger brothers.

"Aye, that we do. But we do it in a ring to make money. Boxing is a profession."

Her nose crinkled in doubt. "You're fishermen." She knew he and her uncle went off the island sometimes on the weekends to fight, but other than that they fished the waters of Lakes Huron and Michigan.

"'Tis true. But we box on the side to make money to raise all you weans. But that 'tisn't the topic here. We're talking about you hitting your cousin."

"But Pa, he said you ain't my real pa. He said my real pa is dead as a doornail up there in the post cemetery." She pointed toward the center of the island. "Ian's a liar."

The stricken look that crossed her father's face scared her. But it passed and his expression warmed, so she relaxed.

"He's an eejit. I hate him," she declared, closing her argument.

Pa looked back at the crowd, then at her. "How about we go watch the raising o' the tree?" He held out his hand.

His sudden turnabout surprised and delighted her. She took his hand and they went back to join the townsfolk who were celebrating the coming of that most sacred of holidays, Christmas. Three men worked to secure a tall blue spruce tree into place, right in the middle of the main intersection of their small village, Mackinac Island. It was an apt name for the village as it sprawled along the shore of Mackinac Island in Lake Huron.

Some folks noticed as Cassie and her pa rejoined the gathering, and some smiled at the child. Her fight with her cousin had drawn their attention away from the main attraction, but no one seemed upset or even surprised that the tussle had taken place. Ian and his pa were nowhere in sight.

She surveyed the crowd, glad to see Chief Joe. He would surely understand why she'd slugged a liar, even if the victim was kin. The Odawa chief nodded, letting her know she was still his friend. He wore his famous fringed leather coat – the one he always wore in winter – and his head was covered in a big fur cap that came down over his ears, like the one her pa had on. In fact, most of the men wore the cap brought to these parts by French fur traders who were the first European settlers to the area.

Once the majestic tree stood securely in place and the crowd dispersed, Cassie and Pa moseyed on down the street toward their small house. She looked up at the man by her side, gentle and kind, but still a grown-up who insisted that children behave. Wondering if he felt any lingering anger for her fight, she refrained from her normal jibber-jabber, as Ma called it. They trod through the snow in silence.

When they reached the fallow vegetable garden below Fort Mackinac, he slowed down and looked up at the long white fortress sitting on a hill and sighed as if something up there bothered him. "Cassie Colleen," he said, relieving her tension with the familiar nickname, "as me only daughter you hold a special place in me heart. You ken that, aye?"

"Aye, Pa."

"And I could have ten more daughters – don't go tellin' your ma I suggested that – I could have ten more and you would still be first daughter, the one I loved a'fore anybody else, lassie or laddie."

Cassie liked this conversation. It made her feel warm despite the chill in the air, as if a blanket of love had been wrapped around her. But there was something odd about what her father said, as if he felt a need to reassure her of his affection. Of course she knew he loved her. He was her pa.

"Your ma and me, we love each o' our children special in their own way because each one o' you is a holy soul all your own. Nobody else can e'er be like you …"

He went on but was losing her. Her attention kept getting diverted by passersby saying hello. She would wave and Pa would nod and greet them, and then he'd go right back to talking. When snowflakes the size of half dollars began to fall – the chief had one of those coins and sometimes showed it around for all to ogle – she tried to catch some of the big flakes on her tongue. But Pa told her to pay attention. So she dutifully stuck her tongue back in her trap. A white rabbit hopped across their path and left pretty tracks in the snow. She pointed that out, but Pa didn't seem impressed. By the time Mr. Doherty, the livery driver, rode by in his dray, which was filled with evergreen boughs women liked to use to decorate their houses for Christmas, Pa had thankfully given up yapping.

When they reached home, he paused before opening the door. "We need to talk more 'bout this with your ma this evening after the laddies have gone to bed."

His tone was soothing, so she wasn't too worried. Maybe a little lickin' was coming for hitting Ian, but it wouldn't be bad. After all, it was a small price to pay for pointing out that her cousin was a liar. Saying her pa wasn't her pa. Ian would surely burn in hell for such slander.

CHAPTER 2

*A*utumn, 2023

As gently as if handling a new-born babe, Wanda McIntyre lifted the ornate vintage dress out of the old steamer trunk. Frayed lace hung by threads and a sash sagged along the waistline. Still, it was a beautiful garment. The light in the attic – two single bulbs dangling from the ceiling – wasn't great but intricate pearl beadwork managed to shine. Shoving her long auburn hair out of her face to get a better look, she handled the garment reverently, stunned that such a treasure had been in the attic all this time.

She jumped when deafening thunder rumbled overhead. The small oval window under the eaves at the end of the attic revealed that darkness prevailed on what had started out as a bright autumn day. Wanda had been up there so long she'd completely lost track of time. It was a charming respite, despite the storm. Perhaps even heightened by the storm.

A bolt of blinding lightning illuminated the window in the few seconds she glanced that way. The room went stark white, and she blinked to get her bearings. The overhead lightbulbs sputtered then came back to life. Rain suddenly pelted the roof.

But Wanda refused to be deterred.

She held the dress up by its shoulders and found it to be heavy. It appeared to be from the late 1800s or early 1900s, being a Victorian-era style. Its yellowed satin would have been crisp white; the scooped lace bodice would have graced a young woman's delicate neck; the voluminous skirt would have rustled when she walked.

As she pulled it out of the trunk and fabric kept coming and coming, her guess became reality. "Look at this! It's a wedding dress with a long train."

There was no one to look unless she counted the ghosts she suspected of lingering in the lovely three-story Victorian-era cottage on Mackinac Island she shared with her husband James.

More thunder and lightning struck, as if telling her something about this treasure. The rain intensified, insistent that she pay attention to the story in that trunk.

She'd been going through the cluttered attic little by little since she'd moved there at Christmastime the year before when she married James, who'd bought the place on the West Bluff of Mackinac Island. Although it was tradition to call the homes on the island "cottages," many like this one were large. With its living room, study, dining room, kitchen, pantry, six bedrooms, five bathrooms, unused servants' quarters, cellar, front and back porches, and flower garden it could hardly be called simple. As with many cottages, stables for horses and a carriage sat out back, although they didn't own any.

Built during the Gilded Age in the latter part of the 1800s, such cottages lined the East and West Bluffs and the main part of town. Queen Anne, Shingle, Stick, and Carpenter Gothic – Wanda had learned they were called in terms of architectural style. The iconic, historic homes and the fact that automobiles were not allowed on the island – options were walking, bicycling, riding a horse, or riding a horse-drawn carriage – made Mackinac Island *Travel and Leisure Magazine*'s "Best Island to Visit in the Country." Wanda adored calling it home with the love of her life after twenty-four unhappy years with her ex.

This was the last of the two big trunks that were in the attic. She'd already gone through the other and found it to be full of dusty and

6

decaying books from the late 1800s and early 1900s, spending more time reading than sorting. *Wuthering Heights, Dracula,* and *The Picture of Dorian Gray* were impossible to resist. She'd settled into an antique wingback chair and read to her heart's content, despite the dim light.

When she turned to this trunk, she'd expected more books and was delighted at this discovery. "Who did this belong to?" she asked the air. Or the ghosts. "Who did she marry? Was she happy? Is she the one who read all those books?" Questions rattled around in her head. This might be a tough mystery to solve, as this woman's history was completely unknown to her. She couldn't wait to try to find out.

She ignored her phone when it sang its merry tune, not wanting her magical treasure hunt to be interrupted. When the little contraption persisted, however, she pulled it out of her apron pocket and checked the screen. She punched it on.

"Alexandra, you won't believe what I just found in my attic." She skipped small talk and got straight to the good part she knew her friend would appreciate. "A vintage wedding dress!"

She put the phone on speaker and set it down so she could continue to examine the enchanting garment.

"Really? Fantastic!" Alexandra's exclamation echoed through the vast space.

Alexandra, a genealogist, loved nothing more than historical and vintage finds. She'd helped Wanda with her family tree, one that led all the way back to an Odawa and French woman named Gichigama Geneviève St. Croix McIntyre, an islander born in 1815. They'd traced Gichigama's marriages to an American soldier who died and then an Irish fisherman, and a passel of children including a daughter named Cassandra who was Wanda's five-times great-grandmother.

Wanda also enjoyed helping Alexandra with her clients' family research projects. The two women had spent many an hour together scouring through records of the deceased. She joined Alexandra on "dead people prowls," as they called them, whenever she wasn't off on an adventure with James, whose job as a photojournalist took him to places around the globe four times a year.

"I'll be over as soon as the storm passes," Alexandra said. "But get ready, my friend. Have I got news for you. I just got a call from a new client who appears to have connections to the very house you're sitting in."

"Really?" Wanda put down the dress and picked up the phone, curiosity getting the better of her.

"Really. There could be a connection to that dress. I'll be there soon."

They clicked off. Wanda sat there staring at the wedding dress. Heritage. Lives from the past. They'd been real people, just like her. She fingered the dress. Touching the fabrics that touched the skin of someone from so long ago felt surreal. It brought the past to life.

She stood up, carefully placed the wedding gown over a second wingback chair, and went downstairs to put on the kettle and start a batch of white chocolate and cherry cookies, Alexandra's favorites. Although, she couldn't pretend they were only for her friend. They were her favorites, too.

Peering out the window over the kitchen sink she could see a break in the charcoal gray clouds off in the distance. Blasts of lightening showed that the backyard's quaint Victorian garden sagged under the weight of the heavy rain. But Wanda knew it would perk up again the moment the sun came out. It was a lovely garden this time of year with blue and pink and white hydrangeas galore, yellow and gold mums, and mature maple and oak trees in variegated autumn shades of orange, red, and gold. There were lush bushes she had yet to name that had turned deep purple. It all made her wonder why she'd ever lived anywhere else but here.

Shaking her head, she realized she'd been in the attic for so long she'd lost track not only of time but the rest of the world, too. It felt jarring, coming back to reality. But the view from her kitchen window helped with the adjustment.

James came into the room, wrapped his arms around her waist from behind, and looked out the window with her. "I guess we could've checked our phones to see if rain was coming. But I find that technology gets away from me here on the island."

"Mackinac Island does that to a person. Isn't it wonderful?" She turned around in his arms.

They kissed and then he twirled her around in rhythm to imaginary music. She molded to his movements, reveling in the joy of the moment. A man – a good man – wooing and appreciating and loving her. There had been times in her life when she'd thought it would never happen, thought she had to settle for less than what she deserved. Less than what any decent woman deserved.

There was no "settling" here.

After twenty-four years with a thankless, self-centered cad, she'd divorced and magically found the love of her life here on the island. The miracle of it still felt new every single day.

He spun her around and she laughed, but a noise stopped them in their dancing tracks.

"Did somebody knock on our door?" he asked.

"I thought I heard something. Surely no one is out in this storm." She slipped out of his arms, padded to the front hall, and opened the door a crack to check.

"Hello Aunt Wanda."

Wanda blinked in disbelief. Her sixteen-year-old niece stood on the porch. It was one of those moments when everything was out of sync, the wrong person in the wrong place at the wrong time. Her sweet, innocent, young niece Madison, soaked to the gills.

"Ohmygod, honey, come in!" She hustled the girl inside as her husband came up behind her. "Madison, this is my husband, James McIntyre. James, this is my niece, Madison Martin."

James did an admirable job of keeping his jaw from falling to the floor. "Madison, come in, come in." Frantically, he motioned toward the stairs. "We need to get you into some dry clothes."

The girl stood there with her auburn hair, which matched the color of her aunt's, matted to her skull, a balky dress and jean jacket clinging to her body, and sneakers squishing water. She had nothing with her except a pitiful purse. No umbrella, no baggage, no extra clothes, no preparation for this visit.

More shocking, she either had a beachball under her dress or was seriously pregnant.

The married couple exchanged a pitying glance. The unexpected visit had the potential to change not only their plans for their upcoming trip but their very lives.

"Let's get you dry." Wanda put an arm around her beloved niece's shoulders and the teen began to weep. Wanda had to lean over the big belly to embrace the girl. The poor kid cried it out while dripping rainwater all over the hall floor and soaking her aunt in the process.

James fetched tissues, Madison dried her eyes, and only then did she become aware of the mess she'd made. "Oh, I'm sorry. I got everything all wet. I'm such a klutz. I'll clean it up."

"No harm done," James insisted. "Nothing that can't be fixed."

"Come on, sweetheart. We'll go upstairs where both of us can change into something warm and dry." Wanda guided Madison up the hall stairs.

Wanda glanced back at James, who watched in stunned disbelief like a man who'd just been told he had a secret child he'd never known about.

CHAPTER 3

*C*hristmastime, 1837

"Cassie Colleen, you know how much I love you."

Pa had already told her that a hundred times that day. She knew he loved her and was glad for it, but he was getting boring. "Ah huh," she droned as she shoved a wayward lock of her long black hair with its auburn highlights off her face and behind her ear. "I love you, too," she politely replied for the tenth time. She was anxious to get down to it. If Pa wanted to whup her behind, fine. Get it over with.

She, Pa, and Ma sat at the table, winter wind noisily whipping around outside. A fire blazed in the large fireplace used for cooking and warmth. Their clapboard house had one large living area, a bedroom for her parents, a smaller bedroom for Pa's ma, Mamo to her grandchildren, and a loft where the kids slept. Her three younger brothers were snoozing away up there at that very moment. Mamo always went to sleep early. An outhouse sat twenty feet outside the back door.

Uncle Niall, Aunt Saoirse, and their kids, including that pesky Ian, lived next door. Their house was much the same minus the bedroom for Mamo. She was from Ireland and didn't speak much proper English, so her grandchildren often interpreted for her. Cassie especially liked helping her out, as the old woman returned the favor with wonderful Irish stories.

Cassie loved her other grandmother, too, her ma's ma. She often went to work with Ma at Madame La Framboise's large house, the home of the Odawa woman who'd married a French fur trader and was one of the wealthiest people on the island. Cassie liked Madame La Framboise, who loved children and made sure they had everything they needed to attend the Mission School so they'd be educated. Cassie loved school.

Ma was a cook alongside her own mother at Madame's house, where her grandmother lived and where her ma had been raised. Ma had recently taken on other responsibilities in the house, like managing guests and arranging big dinners and buying supplies. Cassie knew her ma was smart like that.

So Cassie got to spend a lot of time with that grandmother, too, as well as the one who lived with her. Being an Odawa who married a French fur trader, a grandfather Cassie had never met because he died before she was born, her maternal grandmother had always been called Grandmère. It was easy that way to keep her grandmothers separate. The Irish Mamo and the Odawan Grandmère.

It was the only life the girl knew, family surrounding her like a comfy nest. Yet somehow she understood that not all children got to grow up close to so many people who loved them. Except for that Ian, of course. He didn't count.

Ian. Ah, yes. It was time to get down to it. "Pa, if you're gonna give me a lickin' for hitting Ian, I don't think it's fair. But please don't talk anymore. Go ahead and do it."

She stood up, ready to take her punishment, a brave Irish warrior goddess like the ones Mamo told stories about. Boudica was her favorite, although the pirate queen Gracie O'Malley was a close second. Cassie treasured being half Irish along with her Odawa and French heritage.

"Sit down, lassie. You're naw gettin' a lickin'."

Flabbergasted, she plopped down in her chair.

Ma said, "This isn't about Ian, love. I have a story to tell you. When

I'm done, your pa has another story to add to it. Do you understand? You must listen carefully."

Ma's braided black hair shimmered in the dancing light of the fire. Cassie imagined Irish fairies flitting about spraying Ma with magic dust. In fact, she'd believed the fairies lived amongst them ever since Mamo told her so. Mamo said the Tuatha de Danaan were the first people in Ireland a long, long time ago, and after a big war they became wee folk, fairies, with magical powers. Cassie knew that fairies had come with her Irish family to Mackinac Island because she could see them.

Once after Mamo finished a fairy story, Ian privately told Cassie that was just a silly story. The fairies weren't real. She only thought she saw them because she had a wild imagination.

Cassie hated Ian. He spoiled everything.

Now, sitting at the table with her parents and finding out she wasn't going to be punished for hitting the spoiler, she fretted. Apparently more grownup talking was coming her way. If they started that love thing again… Her mother broke into her thoughts.

"I was fifteen years old when I met your pa here. It was the very day he arrived on the island from Ireland."

"I know, Ma. I've heard this story."

"You must listen, child." Ma's voice took on a stern edge but mellowed again. "There's a new part to the story. You know that we looked at each other and fell in love like that." She snapped her fingers. Ma and Pa smiled at each other like they always did at that part of the story. They looked back at Cassie. "What you don't know is that I had been married before, but my husband died. He was an American soldier at the fort. He died of the flu. Do you know what that is?"

Cassie nodded. She knew people who'd had it, but they didn't die.

"He's buried," Ma said, "in the post cemetery. You see, my love, I had a baby then, a little girl."

"Really?" This was quite an astonishing development. Cassie's heartbeat quickened with excitement. A sister! "Where is she?"

Her parents exchanged another glance.

"Cassie Colleen, me love," Pa said, his voice soft and kind, "she's right here."

He took her hand. Ma took her other hand.

She didn't understand. Turning in her seat one way and then the other, she looked for her sister. None appeared.

"My love," Ma said, "that baby was ... "

"No!" Cassie screamed. Her mind swirling and heart racing, she yanked her hands away from them. "Wait. Wait. That's not me, is it? No. It can't be me. You're my pa." She pointed at the only father she'd ever known.

Their pathetic, silent stares answered. Frantic, she leapt out of her chair. Yelling "No! No!" she raced around the room, not knowing what to do.

Her brothers' heads popped up over the side of the loft. "What's wrong, Sissy?" one of them asked.

Eyes wild as a trapped animal's and glistening with tears, she glared up at her brothers, then at the two liars in front of her. They'd known this all her life and never told her. Ma and that man she'd always thought was her pa stood up, arms outstretched, beseeching her to calm down. Ma almost got ahold of her arm but she got to the door and ran out into the blistering cold night before they could catch her.

In an instant she disappeared in the cover of heavily falling snow, a thick cloak rendering her invisible to those who sought her.

The voices of Ma and that man yelling her name faded away as she headed for her private place in the center of the island. She had no plan other than to get to her cave. She was freezing cold, not having bothered to snatch her coat. But that didn't matter. She needed to get away from those liars.

Trekking uphill through a foot of newly fallen snow in her regular shoes instead of boots, her feet quickly felt dead. Blinded by white, she sobbed tears that froze on her eyelashes. Her ears stung so badly it felt like they'd been immersed in scolding hot water. She went as far as she could, refusing to admit defeat, but eventually knew she wouldn't make it to her cave. It was too far. Her violently shivering body and chattering teeth implored her to go home.

It was then he appeared out of nowhere, a snowy white vision like in a fable. At first, she thought it might be an Odawa warrior like in Chief Joe's stories, or maybe a Tuatha de Danaan warrior like Mamo described. But her cousin Ian stepped out of the cloud of white. He carried a patchwork blanket of animal furs – rabbit, squirrel, and racoon – and wrapped it around her small body. She clasped it closed tight in front and nearly fainted from its blessed warmth. He took the fur hat off his head and tugged it onto hers, making sure it covered her ears.

She couldn't speak, but when he put an arm around her shoulders and turned her toward home, she readily let him guide her down the hill. When they neared town, Cassie could see that the whole village seemed to be outside looking for her, calling her name, lanterns held high in pursuit like flitting fireflies in the winter night. A large fire on the shore sent sparkling cinders shooting into the sky only to fizzle out in falling snow. It was quite a sight to behold.

Chief Joe was the first to see the two youngsters plodding down the hill. He hollered at the others, and adults scampered toward them. They stepped away, however, when Ma and Pa got there. Without a word, her pa picked her up and carried her home.

Once in the house, Pa set Cassie down by the fire and he stepped aside. Mamo held up a shawl for privacy as Ma stripped off her child's wet clothes and shoes. Ma wiped down Cassie's naked body with a cloth, and Mamo wrapped her grandchild in the warm wool shawl while Pa fetched a flannel nightgown. Ma pulled the nightgown on over Cassie's head, and Mamo rewrapped the shawl around the child. Pa fetched a cup and Ma filled it with hot cider from a pot that hung at the side of the fire. Best of all, no one said a word.

Cassie had never felt more loved in her life.

She wondered where Ian had gone. He'd disappeared. She supposed she should thank him. It was possible he'd saved her life.

A short while later, Mamo kissed Cassie's cheek and returned to her room. Ma and Pa followed Cassie up the ladder to the kids' sleeping loft. Ma swaddled her up like a papoose in wool blankets and quilts on her straw-filled mat. Her brothers stared wide-eyed from their mats. She was surprised when Ma and Pa sat down on either side of her.

"You didna get a chance to hear me part o' the story yet," Pa said. She listened intently this time. "Cassie Colleen, when I took that long, arduous journey across the ocean sea and down a long river and o'er those grand lakes and finally landed on our island here, it felt like I'd come to the end o' the earth. But then I got out o' that canoe and who is the first islander I see?" He smiled at Ma. "Gichi, the most beautiful woman I'd e'er laid me sorry eyes on. I knew then I'd come to the right place. This was going to be me home, and I was going to have a family. You see, one o' the first things she told me was she had a bairn. A sweet little girl named Cassandra." He tapped a forefinger on the tip of Cassie's nose. "I was o'erjoyed! I couldna believe me luck. Not only was I getting a wife, I was getting a daughter, too. It doesna matter that I wasn't here on the day you were born. You've been me daughter from the day I arrived on the island and you'll be me daughter until the day I die. I love you, Cassie Colleen." He kissed her forehead.

"As do I," Ma said, stroking and kissing her hair.

"That was a good story, Pa," Cassie's oldest brother Sean said.

"Ah huh," the younger boys agreed as they snuggled into their blankets.

"Now everybody go to sleep," Ma said, sounding like she did every night, normalcy slipping back into their lives.

As her parents scuttled over to the ladder, Cassie whispered, "I love you, too, Ma and Pa."

"Good night, mon bébé." Ma climbed down the ladder.

"Good night, Cassie Colleen. You laddies, too," Pa said as he went down and disappeared from sight.

"Hey Cassie," Sean whispered. "Do you love us, too?"

All three boys tittered.

"Oh go to sleep, you hooligans."

They settled down and became quiet until she softly said, "Aye, you know I love you hooligans, too."

It was the youngest, three-year-old Little Niall, named after his uncle, who replied. "I wuv you too, Casshie."

Cassie laid there listening as her family fell asleep. Her brothers slept quietly. Pa's soft snoring could be heard through the bedroom door downstairs. Neither Ma nor Mamo made a peep. The fire died down but still crackled, the low flames casting dark shadows about their house.

The place looked different to her now. It was home, yes, but a different home. It was no longer her childish retreat. She'd grown up a lot in the last couple of hours.

No one seemed to care or find it odd that Pa wasn't her real pa. It gulled her that Ian had been right. He wasn't a liar after all.

She wondered about the man who was married to Ma when she was born. What was his name? What did he look like? Where did he come from? He would never feel like her father. That was Pa. A dead soldier in the post cemetery would never be able to take that away from them.

Still, curiosity bubbled up and made her wonder which one of those white crosses in the cemetery was him. There were quite a few, so it would be hard to figure out.

When the weather was better and she had on her warm clothes and boots and it was daytime, she'd visit the cemetery to try to find him. She didn't know why she wanted to know. She just did.

CHAPTER 4

*A*utumn, 2023

Wanda took her niece into the master bathroom. "How about a hot shower?"

"Okay."

"Take off those wet clothes and toss them in the sink." Wanda opened the glass door and reached into the tiled shower to turn on the water. Steam quickly billowed out. She grabbed a couple of fat towels out of the linen closet and hung them over the shower door. "Go ahead and hop in while I find you something to wear."

Her emotions spent, Madison shucked her shoes and yanked off her jacket like an unfeeling robot. She turned her back to take off her dress.

Wanda went into the clothes closet, tore off her wet top, threw it in the hamper, and pulled a clean one on over her head. She exchanged her jeans for dry ones, then went to James's side to grab a broad sweatshirt off the shelf. Back on her side, she had to rustle through a drawer before finding what she wanted, a pair of flannel sweatpants with a drawstring waist. She untied the string and stretched out the waist as far as it would go. Madison was about her height and was normally lithe and athletic, like Wanda had been at that age. Madison was also as ginormous as Wanda had been when pregnant. James's big sweatshirt and the stretched-out sweatpants were sorely needed. She added a pair of fluffy slippers and hurried back to the bathroom.

"Here, honey," she hollered to be heard over the gush of water. Madison had her back to the frosted glass, so Wanda couldn't see the full measure of the girl's pregnancy. "Your clothes are right here." She laid the dry clothes on the counter and took the wet things out of the sink – jacket, dress, and scanty panties. Her niece had done her best to wring everything out, but Wanda used a towel to wrap them up so they wouldn't drip all over the floor on the way to the laundry room downstairs. She piled Madison's wet sneakers on top of the stack. "No bra?"

"Nah. They don't fit anymore."

"Ah. Of course. Come downstairs when you're ready. We'll get something to eat."

Madison kept her back turned as she washed.

"She'll have to get over that," Wanda mumbled to herself as she went down the stairs, remembering how many people – doctors, nurses, interns, aides, her husband, her mother, a couple of friends, and probably voyeuring strangers – had ended up seeing her naked pregnant body by the time she gave birth.

"How is she?" James asked nervously. "Is she okay?"

"She seems fine. Just lost, apparently."

He followed her into the laundry room where she plopped the sneakers on top of the dryer and threw the clothes into the washer and started it.

"This is the niece you've told me about," he stated. "The one you're so close to."

"Yeah. She used to spend summers with me. My sister isn't exactly mother-of-the-year."

They returned to the living room where he'd lit a fire in the fireplace, welcome warmth to combat the now raging storm outside. It also offered a sense of stable homeyness to the confusing situation inside.

She sat down on the sofa and patted the space beside her. "Thanks for cleaning up the wet floor, sweetheart." She pointed to the hallway where the floor was now dry.

"No problem." James sat down beside her and wrapped an arm around her shoulders. He kissed her forehead. She took his hand and kissed it. "How far along is she?" he asked. "Did she say?"

"No, she hardly talked at all. But I'm guessing about seven months. It's odd that she came to me. I'm glad she did, mind you, but with my kids grown and living in other parts of the country, it's like having one of my own kids in my home again."

"Well, as you know, this is a first for me. My ex refused to have children, so I'm at a total loss here. But I want to do whatever I can to help the poor girl. I can't believe her parents aren't on top of this."

"My sister isn't really on top of anything. So here we are. A teen in our house. A pregnant teen."

They snuggled and sat in silence for a while, taking it all in. They both came to attention, though, when Madison, looking more like twelve than sixteen except for her big belly, waddled down the stairs in her makeshift outfit. The adults stood up, James reaching out as if to carry her into the room. He took her arm as she made her way to a chair and fell in.

"Are you hungry?" Wanda asked. "When was the last time you ate? It's lunchtime. I'll fix us something." There were a hundred pressing questions to ask, but she started with the basics.

"That would be nice. I haven't eaten today."

Wanda started for the kitchen but realized that would leave James in a very awkward situation. He was already standing in the middle of the room looking like he didn't know which way to go. She felt certain he had no idea what to say to a pregnant teenager who'd shown up out of the blue. For him, that would be like trying to talk to a Martian. Actually, an alien would be easier than a teen. He grasped her thought.

"How about I go make us some sandwiches?" he suggested. "I can bring them back in here and we'll eat by the fire."

Rain pummeled the windows. The charcoal sky had darkened to coal. And a chill made the fireplace a magnet for comfort.

"Perfect." Wanda marveled at her husband's astuteness, something she hadn't been accustomed to in her former marriage.

Once he was out of earshot, she moved to the chair next to her niece and took her hand. "Okay. Spill. What's up? I had no idea you were pregnant. My sister doesn't tell me anything."

The story tumbled out like a bad heartbreaker movie. *Baby Daddy Gone*. All too common, all too predictable, it was a tawdry love-gone-wrong tale of yet another young woman who'd fallen in love, had sex, and was subsequently abandoned by the father of her child.

"Gavin's eighteen. He graduated last spring and is in college now," Madison explained. "He's got a football scholarship at State. He says he doesn't have time for a baby."

"But you do? Hmph. The scoundrel."

"Aunt Wanda, he said he loved me and wanted to marry me after I graduated."

"Yeah, I'm afraid they always say that."

"I'm scared. I don't know how to have a baby."

"Oh, sweetie. Nobody does with the first one. I didn't know, either, until I had my first. Do you know ..." she let go of Madison's hand and gestured "... that we have an ancestor who had a baby when she was only fifteen? Right here on the island. I've done research on our family history. We come from strong stock, my love. Gichigama Geneviève St. Croix McIntyre. They called her Gichi. She was the daughter of a Native American Odawa woman and French fur trader. She married a soldier at the fort with English heritage and had their daughter Cassandra – they called her Cassie – when she was fifteen. That was common back then, and the young mothers survived. Why by sixteen Gichi had been married to the American, had Cassie, was widowed, remarried an Irishman, and was pregnant again."

Madison thought that over. "So ... so you're saying I'm a real slacker compared to my ancestor Gichi."

They laughed and Wanda was delighted to see a bit of humor spill out of her niece who'd always been a lot of fun. How she managed that with her stodgy parents, Wanda had never known.

"Ah, now, don't go comparing yourself to anybody thinking you have to keep up," Wanda teased, patting Madison's knee. "But seriously, honey, billions of teenagers throughout all times have had babies and come through it just fine. You will, too. I'm absolutely sure of it."

"My mom isn't so sure. She acts like I'm gonna die and I deserve it."

"Oh hell, that sounds like her. Do your parents know you're here?"

"Nah. I didn't tell them I was coming. They think I'm at my friend's for the weekend. She's the only friend I have left. All the rest think I'm a slut because I'm pregnant."

"How did you get here?"

"My friend drove me to the ferry."

"Ah, about a forty-five-minute drive from Petoskey." Madison's hometown was on Little Traverse Bay on Lake Michigan. "That was nice of her."

Madison went on to explain that her dad, the controlling brother-in-law Wanda had never liked, was furious that she'd hidden the pregnancy until it was too late for an abortion. Madison didn't want an abortion. Her mom, she said, simply cried a lot.

"I can't take it anymore, Aunt Wanda. They just stare at me all the time, like I'm a werewolf who's invaded their home. I want my dad to shut up about how much I've disappointed them. And I can't stand mom's boo-hooing anymore. It's like she thinks she accidentally got pregnant by a vampire or something."

Wanda squeezed her hand. That sounded exactly like her sister. Everything had always been about her. Walking a mile, or one step, in someone else's shoes had never occurred to her.

"What about school?" Wanda wanted to know. It was October. School had started the first week of September.

"I didn't go this year. It's too embarrassing. When school was out last May and I told Gavin I thought I was pregnant, he stopped talking to me. He said I ruined his life because I got pregnant. He hates me. He told everybody and said it was my fault." Tears welled in her eyes.

"Bastard. As if he didn't have anything to do with it."

James appeared with a full tray and made small talk while Wanda got up to put out three TV trays. He passed out the chow. Then he took drink orders and returned to the kitchen. Madison ate like a bear coming out of hibernation, her sandwich half gone by the time James got back with three glasses and a pitcher of iced tea.

The adults watched in awe as the teen devoured her food – a chicken sandwich, chips, and pickles. She downed her tea and refilled her glass.

Wanda and James took more time to finish their meals, during which Madison asked if she could go get the bag of chips. Wanda nodded assent and the girl shoved herself out of her chair and shuffled off. She came back with her hand in the bag and her mouth full. She'd downed half the bag by the time her hosts were done. Then she went and got the pickles, dipping her fingers in and eating out of the jar.

James was the first to broach the subject of the elephant in the room. An expectant pachyderm at that. "Madison, I know this is difficult, but I heard you say your parents don't know where you are. Should they be called? They might be worried."

The teen shrugged. "Maybe."

"I'll do it," Wanda offered. "If they get mad at me, they know I don't give a rat's ass."

She left the room, went into the kitchen, and could be heard dialing her phone. Madison and James leered at one another.

He was the first to crack. "You doing okay? Can I get you anything else to eat?"

The girl tossed out a sliver of a grin. "Nah. Thanks." She set the pickle jar down on the side table and wiped the acrid juice off her fingers with her napkin.

Wanda's voice escalated in the kitchen. "I don't give a .... She ... support right now ..."

She faded in and out, so the living-roomers only caught bits and pieces of her conversation. But they could tell it wasn't going well.

When Wanda returned, her face was flushed and jaw set, she held her phone in a death grip. "You're staying here." She addressed Madison then looked at James apologetically. They hadn't had time to discuss that in private.

"Of course," he said. "Stay as long as it takes. Oh. Huh. I mean, you know, until … you do whatever you need to do. I have no idea what I'm talking about, do I? I've never been around someone who's having a baby."

Wanda and Madison exchanged a glance and burst into laughter.

"Neither have I," Madison mused. "Neither have I."

There was one more question that needed to be addressed, but Wanda decided to save it until later. What did Madison plan on doing after the baby was born? Try to find a way to support it and keep it? Put it up for adoption? Give it away?

The aunt didn't ask yet because she suspected her niece had no answer.

CHAPTER 5

hristmastime, 1837

Wintertime sunshine was different from in the summer. It struck newly fallen snow with a brilliance like nothing else on earth, creating a field of dazzling diamonds scattered atop a blanket of white. That was one of the reasons, although she also loved the other seasons, winter was Cassie's favorite. This morning was especially enchanting.

She stood on the lane staring at the crosses in the post cemetery. Only the tops were visible in the deep snow. There was no way to tell which one was the man Ma had been married to when she was born. She went through the gate anyway and wiped snow off a few, trying to decipher names. None were familiar. Giving up, she turned to go.

Ma stood at the gate. She wore the long mink cloak she'd had for as long as Cassie could remember and had her red wool hat pulled down over her ears and tied under her chin with a ribbon. She carried her red wool muff lined with rabbit fur. Her dark beauty was striking against the winter white scene surrounding her.

Without a fuss, Ma silently walked to the back of the cemetery, nodded toward a cross, and said, "That one." She didn't bother to take a hand out of its warm muff to point.

Surprised by her ma's willingness, Cassie hesitated before swiping snow away to read the cross. She was an advanced reader for her age and had no trouble with it. "Harold Smith."

"Aye. He was a private in the Army, stationed at the fort."

"Huh." Cassie cocked her head to study the name. "Harold Smith. Isn't that English?"

"Aye."

"You married an Englishman?" Cassie gasped. That seemed impossible. The Irish – her own Irish family – despised the English for all the injustices they'd thrust upon their homeland of Eire.

"His parents were English and moved to this country before he was three. He was American."

Cassie wasn't having it. She knew that heritage mattered, having been taught that all her life. "How could you marry an Englishman?"

Ma paused. It was a difficult question for her. "It isn't a matter of what country a person is from. It's a matter of his character. Heart. And soul." Her voice faltered. Her eyes clouded with sorrow.

Cassie thought her ma hadn't liked that Englishman very much. She hadn't liked that man's heart and soul. Did that mean he hadn't been good to her? That was a question she wasn't brave enough to ask.

As if reading her thoughts, Ma said, "One of the best things that ever happened to me was when I was married to Harold Smith, because I had you. My first child. I was the happiest woman alive."

Cassie felt certain her mother was leaving out big parts of the story. She decided to let it rest. She didn't really want to know.

They walked together, snow crunching underfoot as they made their way down the hill to town. Ma didn't say anything, so Cassie refrained from jibber-jabbering.

Mesmerized by the beauty of the spectacular winter day, she let herself become one with the earth the way Chief Joe said all humans should do. He said white men didn't know how to be one with the earth, and he complimented Cassie on her ability to do so even though her skin was almost white. She'd been supremely honored by the praise.

When they reached their front door, she and Ma stamped snow off their boots and used the broom left outside for the purpose to sweep off the rest. Inside Cassie found her Uncle Niall and cousin Ian sitting at the table with Pa, her brothers, and Mamo. All eyes glommed onto her and Ma as they came in. Ma greeted the company as she and Cassie took off their coats and hats and hung them on the pegs by the door.

"What, may I ask, is going on?" Ma said jovially. She knew the answer to her own question.

"Come, sit, please," Pa requested.

Both females joined the crew of males and the family matriarch at the table.

Mamo turned her attention to Ian with a silent glare. Obviously, the grandmother had orchestrated whatever was about to occur. Everyone followed her lead and stared at Ian.

Ian cleared his throat and nervously ran a finger around the collar of his Sunday shirt, which normally would have been changed after mass but was still worn for this occasion. "Cassie, I, ah ... I ..." He glanced at his pa, who nodded. "Cassie," he said, starting over, "I apologize for saying what I said. I don't know why I did it. It wasn't my place to tell you. Ma and Pa didn't know I knew. I'm sorry."

He looked at Mamo, who nodded approval, then at his father, who did the same. He let out of sigh of relief. He'd done well, but there was more.

The boy finished off his practiced speech. "Aunt Gichi and Uncle Liam, I'm sorry to you, too."

Cassie couldn't tell if her cousin was sincere or only saving his hide. In either case, she felt ambivalent about it. Now that she knew the truth, there would never be any going back, so the apology didn't matter.

"Ian," Pa said, "how did you know? Did you overhear one of us ..." he pointed at the adults "... talking about it?"

Ian shook his head. "Nah. Otis Redman told everybody at school. He heard his parents talking about it. He was gonna tell her when we got back after Christmas."

Cassie was dumbstruck. All the kids at school knew about this? There was a whole world out there that hadn't included her? For the first time in her life, she felt like an outsider on her own island.

Silence loomed as everyone took that in. The fire snapped. A horse trotted by outside.

"The truth is, mon petit minou," Ma finally spoke, falling into her native French as she addressed her daughter, "we should have told you sooner. Something like this was bound to happen."

"I'm your pa, and that's that." Pa slapped the table. "I love you, Cassie Colleen."

Cassie grinned. "I know, Pa. I love you, too."

Ian became noticeably restless as the conversation turned mushy. "Can we go now, Pa?" he asked his own father.

"Aye, mac. After a proper goodbye," his pa said.

The boy popped up out of his seat. "'Bye Mamo. 'Bye Aunt Gichi and Uncle Liam." He dashed to the door, grabbed his coat, flung the door open to a blast of cold air, and shot outside without bothering to don his coat. He'd make it to his house next door without it.

Niall McIntyre, more prudent than his son, bundled up. He kissed his mother's cheek and said goodbye to everyone.

When he was gone and the Liam McIntyre family was left at the table, six-year-old Sean said, "Ma, Pa, do I have a dead pa in the post cemetery?"

His father rustled his copper hair. "Nae, nae. There are no more dead pa's in the cemetery."

The boys wanted to go ice fishing, a Sunday afternoon favorite in the wintertime. So the males put on their heavy wear, grabbed their fishing gear, and were off. Ma left to deliver a basket of food to a poor family.

That left the youngest and oldest females in the family alone. They moved to the fireside, Mamo in her rocking chair and Cassie on a stool. Mamo knitted a pair of mittens for Little Niall, as he had a habit of losing his. They could only be worked on when he wasn't home, as they were his Christmas present. She was securing the "bairn string," a knitted rope. Each end would be sewn onto a mitten, then the middle of the string would be sewn onto the inside collar of his coat. The string would be threaded through the sleeves, leaving a mitten to dangle out on each side, therefore reassuring the mittens wouldn't go anywhere. At least that was the plan. Little Niall had managed to lose the last ones anyway.

Cassie always felt secure with Mamo knitting or cooking or simply being. One of the things she loved most about being alone with her elder was that she wasn't expected to talk. Silence worked well for both. Cassie stared into the flames, lost in thought.

Mamo finished the mittens and held them up by the string. Cassie grinned. She still had to wear a bairn string. It would be a rite of passage to outgrow it. Although, she already felt as if she'd gone through a rite of passage, like the ones Chief Joe told about for the Odawa.

"Mamo, do you ken Chief Joe's story about the pimada … pimadaz … I forget what it's called. It's a great story."

Mamo placed her knitting in the basket of yarn on the floor at her side, clasped her hands in her lap, and said, "Aye. I ken the story well. Chief Joe is a grand seanchaí." Cassie knew that meant a great story-teller. "'Tis pimadaziwin that he tells aboot, a time when a pearsa goes alone into the fásach – what do ye call that in yer English?"

"Wilderness."

"Aye. Or the cladach or the bharr conic." She raised her eyebrows, waiting for the translation.

"I think that's the shore and a hilltop."

"Aye. In pimadaziwin a pearsa goes there and waits fer dream visitors to bless their life."

"Aye, 'tis that." Cassie naturally fell into Irish vernacular when alone with Mamo.

"We have the same stories in Eire. The Tuatha de Danaan, wee folk, can bring aboot all kinds o' magick. If ye wander into the wilderness, they can bless ye or curse ye."

Cassie contemplated that for a minute. "But you have to be a good pearsa first a'fore they bless you with good magick. Aye?"

"Aye, a leanbh."

Cassie reveled in Mamo's term of endearment, although she'd never been quite sure what it meant. All she knew was that "a leanbh" was always spoken with love in the voice.

"Ye feel ye have gone through pimadaziwin?" Mamo's pale blue eyes twinkled with wisdom, wrinkles unfurling from their corners. "Ye went to the ground o' the dead and came home kenning yer life is blessed. Aye?"

Surprised at this revelation, Cassie paused. She hadn't put all those pieces together. "I … I think so. Do you think so?"

"It dinnae matter what I think. 'Tis fer ye alone to decide. Now, would ye like to have a piece o' the apple pie I made a'fore those hooligans get home?"

A wide smile lit up Cassie's face. She might have doubts about many things but had no doubt she was blessed with the best mamo on earth.

CHAPTER 6

utumn, 2023

James covered Madison with a quilt. The pregnant teen slept like a zombie on the sofa in the living room. The storm had subsided and stillness surrounded them, creating perfect conditions for nap time. He quietly added a log to the fire to make sure the room stayed cozy warm, then joined his wife in the kitchen. He poured each of them a lemonade – no alcohol in this house, as neither of them imbibed – while she stacked their lunch dishes in the dishwasher. She added soap, closed it up, and started the machine.

"Let's go into your study to talk," she suggested, taking the glass he offered.

He led the way into the room she'd decorated for him in earthy greens and golds, natural woods, and cushy furniture meant for relaxing as well as work. A triad of windows on the outer wall filled the room with light. A long antique wood table covered the length of one wall, with open wood shelves above it. The table was strewn with photographs while the shelves held a variety of camera equipment.

James's job as a photojournalist was entirely of his own making. He didn't have to work at all, having come from a wealthy oil and gas family in Texas. He could sit on his behind and do nothing for the rest of his life if he chose. But he had a passion, a calling, to photograph the world and its people and reveal their grandeur to themselves and to others. His aim was for all people everywhere to know and understand one another, to see each other as equally valuable inhabitants of planet Earth. He had an affinity for animals, too, and would take on any he came upon.

As a social media influencer, he had a quarter of a million followers on Instagram and almost that many on Facebook. His photography had won him countless awards. He'd become famous in his field.

A year ago, when Wanda first met him and so quickly fell in love, she hadn't known any of that. He'd simply been a guy who liked to take pictures and who treated her with loving respect. His talent, wealth, and worldly benevolence were bonuses she never expected.

They sat down together on the loveseat, each sipping their drinks.

"Obviously," he said, "we can't go on our trip next week."

"Honey, I've been thinking it over, and I think you should go. I'll stay here."

They debated for a while, but Wanda knew he'd looked forward to a trip to Antarctica for years. This was the time of year to go, autumn in the Northern Hemisphere and spring in the Southern Hemisphere. If he didn't go now, he'd have to wait another year. He'd been like a little kid at Christmas planning for it. She insisted he go. Finally, he relented.

"The trip is three weeks long," he observed. "I hope I'm home before the baby comes."

He went to his desk to work on his travel plans, and Wanda decided to make cookies in anticipation of Alexandra's visit, which she'd almost forgotten about in all the chaos. Her friend would be there any minute.

Twenty minutes later Alexandra came in the back door without knocking, seeing she'd become like family. "I smell cookies!" The older woman hollered as she barreled into the kitchen at the very moment Wanda took the first batch out of the oven. Alexandra cheered, "My favorites! Cherry and white chocolate."

"They need to cool," Wanda said as she took them off the tray with a spatula and piled them onto a plate.

Alexandra grabbed a small one, tossed it from hand to hand, blew on it, and popped the whole thing into her mouth. "Oh yum!" she said after swallowing hard. "These can't be beat. Come here. You deserve a hug."

The two women embraced as Wanda chuckled at her friend's antics. Alexandra snarfed down another cookie before her hostess could get a word out. Alexandra, a native islander, was a colorful widow in her seventies.

"I know you have something important to tell me about this house," Wanda said as she spooned cookie dough onto the cookie sheet. "But first, I have to tell you who showed up here today. You won't believe it. It's ..."

"Aunt Wanda. Can I have some?" Madison stood in the doorway, a hand resting on her belly. She stared at the plate of cookies like a wild animal eyeing a steak on the grill.

Alexandra's eyes grew wide. She held a cookie midair as she stared.

"Of course, sweetie. Have a seat." Wanda motioned to the full plate with her spoon and her friend got the hint. Alexandra grabbed the plate, went over to the kitchen table, and pulled out a chair.

"Here, sweet pea," the older woman said, placing the plate in front of the chair.

Madison sat down and didn't hesitate to dig in.

"I'm Alexandra, a friend of the family." Alexandra took a chair and snatched another cookie.

"I'm Madison, Aunt Wanda's niece."

"Nice to meet you. Are you staying here to have your baby?"

The oven door slammed closed as Wanda fumbled upon hearing the bold question while she put in another batch.

Madison had no problem with it. "Pro'bly. My parents hate me."

"I see. Huh." Alexandra took napkins out of the holder, slid one over to the teen, then wiped her hands before patting the girl's arm. "Well, you're in good hands here on the island." She looked back at

Wanda questioningly. Wanda nodded. "They have great medical staff here. In the winter not many people are here, so you'll probably have them all to yourself."

Wanda noticed she skipped the part about how there would most likely only be the year-round doctor and one nurse at the clinic. She knew the medical professionals were more than competent and many babies over the years had been born on the island, which seemed like a special blessing all its own for the beginning of life. But, still, there was no hospital should anything go wrong. When a patient needed a hospital, they were airlifted out and taken to the mainland. She sloughed off the thought. No time to think about that now.

She set the timer for the cookies and asked what they wanted to drink. She still had her lemonade, and Alexandra opted for some of that. Madison politely asked for milk.

Once they were all settled at the table and the empty cookie plate stared up at them, Wanda got back to the reason for Alexandra's visit. "So, pray tell, what did you find that connected to this house? Madison, Alexandra is a genealogist and sometimes she lets me help her."

"Cool." The girl nodded approvingly.

"Yes," Alexandra said, "we lovingly call our searches 'dead people prowls.' And have I got a doozie. My new client is Barb Rand, a seventy-year-old woman from down below – oh, Madison, if you've never heard the expression 'down below,' it means the lower part of the lower peninsula. Not here."

"Oh yeah, I know," Madison told her. "I'm from Petoskey, so we say that. Trolls."

Alexandra chuckled. "That's it. Trolls. They live below the Mackinac Bridge. Anyway, this Barb Rand recently inherited letters written by her grandmother who lived from 1883 to 1978. The return address is this very house. The grandmother's married name was Anne Rand. I looked up the original builder of this house and, sure enough, it was Anne's father, a Chicago architect. This was their family summer home. But when Anne married, he gave the cottage to the couple, apparently as a wedding gift."

Madison looked around. "Nice wedding gift."

36

"It sure is. Our contemporary woman, Barb Rand, has been focusing on records from her ancestors' permanent address in Chicago, but now she's interested in this place, too. She's coming in a couple days and is bringing the letters. We're going to go through the letters and put together the pieces of her family story. Would you like to help?"

"Yeah."

Wanda was surprised but pleased that her niece jumped right in. "Me, too," she said. "This'll be fun. I love old letters."

Alexandra explained, "She hasn't told me yet what's in them. She says I have to read them to understand."

"Oh my. That's interesting," Wanda said.

"Now, what about that dress?" Alexandra asked.

"You won't believe it. It's gorgeous." Wanda got up but motioned for them to stay seated. She checked the timer for the cookies.

Madison said she had to pee before doing anything else. "I have to go every ten minutes," she groaned.

The girl disappeared down the hall.

"So your bratty sister won't take care of her own child while she's pregnant?" Alexandra whispered, her disgust on full display.

"Nope. She won't. Hard to believe but true."

"We'll take care of her. How far along is she?"

"We don't know."

"Has she been to a doctor yet?"

"I don't know that yet either. She's only been here for an hour and a half. I'm taking it slowly."

"Good idea."

The timer dinged and Wanda got out the second batch of cookies. She refilled the plate and both women inhaled another.

"They're so good right out of the oven." Wanda smacked her lips.

"I know. Irresistible."

Madison returned and ate two more.

Wanda motioned toward the attic stairs by the back door. "Let's go look at the wedding dress I found."

Madison grabbed an extra cookie, wrapped it in a napkin, and stuck it in her pocket to take along in case she starved to death on the way. They clomped up two stories of worn wood steps and entered the cavernous space.

"Whew." Alexandra whistled in wonder. "Look at all this stuff. It's like a magic room."

Wanda clicked on the light. The two antique trunks, tattered furniture, weathered suitcases, crumbling boxes, and enough paraphernalia to stock an entire flea market all by itself cluttered the musty, shadowy room. They could hardly worm their way through to the open trunk and wedding dress draped over a chair.

Alexandra lightly ran a finger along the skirt. Madison gently touched the beadwork on the bodice. They all marveled at its intricate, decaying beauty.

"It's like we're spying," Wanda noted, "on somebody's secret life from a long time ago. A young woman wore this very dress on her petite body for what presumably was the most important day of her life."

"I wonder who she was," Madison whispered. "What did she look like? I bet she was beautiful in this dress."

"It brings the dead to life, doesn't it." Turning away from the dress, Alexandra craned her neck toward the trunk. "What else is in there?"

Wanda shrugged. "I don't know. The dress stopped me. Then the storm hit. Then this one came." She pointed at her niece and grinned. "Then we needed cookies."

Alexandra poked her head into the trunk. She backed up and peered in again. "Ah, girls, look at this."

Three heads bowed over the trunk. Three jaws fell in wonder. And three gasps escaped.

"What the heck?" Alexandra held out her hands as if to touch but snatched them back.

"This is gonna be the most fun we've had in the long time," Wanda declared.

"Let's hope so," Alexandra said.

"I need this to get my mind off being fat as a cow," Madison groaned.

"Well, this should do it," Wanda declared. "Come on, let's get this stuff downstairs."

Alexandra held her arm out like a patrol officer at school. "We can do it, Madison. You don't need to be carrying anything down those steep steps."

The two older women loaded up with items from the chest and the three of them worked their way through clutter to the stairs.

"Watch out, Madison," Wanda cautioned. "There's no handrail. Keep your hands on the walls."

"Yes, Aunt Wanda," Madison chortled as they descended. "I know I'm fat and dumb, but I can manage this," she chided.

"You might be fat," her aunt conceded, "but you've never been dumb."

"I got pregnant, didn't I?"

The women couldn't help but chuckle.

Once downstairs, they placed their treasures on the dining room table. Wanda grabbed a cedar hanger from the laundry room and went back up for the wedding dress and its fragile veil. She came back and hung them up over a mirror behind the table.

They stood back and looked at their find, delighted yet mystified.

James came in. "Wow. This is going to keep you busy for a good long while." He joined them in staring.

A knock at the backdoor interrupted and Wanda looked to see who it was. Their next-door neighbor's wizened old face showed through the door window. Alexandra's cousin, Bernard, was a widower retired from a career as an industrial engineer. He'd bought his Queen Anne cottage the year before after visiting Alexandra and falling in love with the island. He especially liked it that his house needed fixing up. His neighbors all appreciated his handyman capabilities, which he generously shared free of charge.

"Come in, Bernard!" Wanda hollered. "In the dining room."

The footfall of work boots caused a racket on the wood floor until the white-haired fellow appeared. A hammer hung from a loop in his overalls and the head of a screwdriver stuck up from one of three narrow pockets on the bib. "I fixed that gate of yours that had a loose hinge ..." He shut up when he saw the vintage wedding dress and the stash on the table. "Oh oh. What have we got here?"

"I don't know," Wanda said, "but we're about to find out. Would you like to help?"

"Of course."

"Okay, let's get started by sorting this out piece by piece. Very, very carefully."

CHAPTER 7

*C*hristmastime, 1837

Cassie stared up at the Christmas tree that stood tall in the middle of Main Street in her village. It was the first one in her life-time, although she'd heard about the tradition of cutting down a tree and decorating it to celebrate the birth of their Lord Jesus Christ. She didn't quite understand the connection, but it was a pretty tree.

Ma told her about such a tree when she was a girl and one again on the day of her marriage to Pa. But the German man who'd intro-duced it had moved away, so there hadn't been one in Cassie's seven years.

Townsfolk decorated the tree with tin stars, strings of popcorn and berries, some of which she and Mamo made, and colorful knitted birds the size of real birds. A big wood cross sat at the very top. Snow had covered it for a few days but on this day before Christmasday, the sun shone down to make its decorations shine. It was quite breathtaking.

Ian came up beside her. "Hey, wanna go up to the fort?"

"I'm looking at the Christmas tree."

"Why?"

"Cuz, silly, it's pretty."

"'Tis just a tree."

"Go away."

"I don't wanna."

"Stop pestering me."

"Nuh uh."

"Go!"

"I ain't goin'."

"You shouldn't say 'ain't.' It ai … isn't a proper word. Besides, I thought you wanted to go to the fort."

"I do. I wanna take the sled so's we can slide down the big hill." He pointed behind them.

She glanced over her shoulder to see his sled sitting there invitingly, begging to be used.

She liked sledding a lot. The problem was it always had to be with Ian, as he'd made the sled himself, the only one on the island. Therefore, he held reign over its use.

The fort he talked about was Fort Hayes, which was inland up a long hill, rather than Fort Mackinac, which was right there in town. It was a perfect winter day for such an adventure – sun shining, powdery snow, no wind. She'd be a moron to refuse.

"Fine," she relented. "But don't talk to me the whole way."

After two hours of sledding up and down and up and down the big hill, they trudged home tired and happy. As they started to part ways so to go to their next-door houses, Ian dropped the rope to his sled and grabbed Cassie's arm.

"Cassie." He spun her around to face him. "I think I wanna marry you when we grow up."

She froze like a rabbit in fear of being trapped. Marriage? How stupid. That was a hundred years away.

"Well, I don't wanna marry you!" She ran into her house and slammed the door.

Pa sat by the fire, smoking his pipe and reading a book. "Did you have a good time, Cassie Colleen?" He asked.

"Yeah. Until the end."

"What happened at the end?"

"Ian wants to marry me."

Her pa laughed so hard he got tears in his eyes. Ma and Mamo came into the room and when he told them, they laughed, too.

Cassie was vexed. She'd learned that word at school when their teacher Mrs. Ferry told her pupils that if they felt "vexed," they were to come talk it over with her. Where was Mrs. Ferry when Cassie needed her?

"It ain't funny!" she declared as she scurried up the ladder to the loft where'd she'd be safe from the silly adults. It was hard to remember good grammar when vexed.

Her anger vanished when the smell of soda bread and plum pudding wafted her way. It was a special night, being Christmas Eve. There would be a big potluck supper at Madame La Framboise's house where Ma and Ma's Ma, Grandmère, worked as cooks. Half the village would be there, including all the McIntyre family. There would be evening mass at Ste. Anne's, and then they would come home to open Christmas presents.

It was an exciting time, as gifts were rare. Cassie had scavenged the woods for sticks she could debark for her brothers for playing stick ball. Pa had loaned her his folding pocketknife to get the job done. Ma and Pa were giving each boy a ball Pa bought down below with money he got from boxing. Cassie made pretty pictures at school for her parents, her best effort at depicting wood scenes. Ma would get the drawing of wildflowers and Pa the one of deer. Well, sorta deer. That one had been harder. Each grandmother, Mamo and Grandmère, was getting a cup of maple syrup Ma helped Cassie tap off trees in the woods. Mamo would love that in her porridge and Grandmère would love it on her buckwheat flapjacks. Cassie couldn't wait to surprise everyone with their gifts.

They all wore their Sunday clothes and bundled up to walk down the street to Madame La Framboise's house, where most of the village gathered to celebrate the birth of Jesus Christ. The feast laid out on the long dining room table was splendid. There was venison, pork, yams, rice, beans, beets, and everything else the girl loved. Some of it had been prepared by Ma and Grandmère. Lots of

43

villagers brought dishes, too. Mamo's soda bread and plum pudding were a big hit.

Everyone was in a celebratory mood. The grownups drank wine and some of the men snuck outside to drink whiskey. With Madame's beautiful home filled with boughs and candles for Christmas, the evening was quite magical.

Madame herself reigned over the event like a majestic queen, wearing a stunning white leather Odawa dress with fringe and intricate green, red, and white beading. She also wore a wide beaded belt that Cassie coveted. Such a belt meant a woman wore her heritage proudly. Cassie would wear one proudly, if she had one, being part Odawa herself.

The girl was in such a good mood she didn't even mind much when stupid Ian told her Happy Christmas.

After supper, Christmas service at Ste. Anne's lasted forever, typical for mass, but eventually the Liam McIntyre family sat around their own fire to open Christmas gifts. Grandmère, who lived at Madame's, had been invited, too. Little Niall fell asleep in Pa's arms while being carried home and had to be roused for the gift giving.

First, the children got their gifts. From Mamo each child got knitted mittens, scarves, and caps made of thick, soft yarn that would keep them comfy and warm outside. Cassie put on the hat and it felt so good, she didn't ever want to take it off. The children all thanked their beloved Mamo, with Little Niall thrusting himself into her lap and gracing her with a sloppy kiss on her cheek, which pleased the old woman no end.

Ma and Pa gave the boys each a ball and Cassie brought out the sticks she made for stickball, one for each boy. She'd hidden them behind the broom because the boys never went near the broom.

Then Cassie got the most amazing gift she'd ever seen.

"It's an Odawa belt!" she exclaimed as she pulled it out of its leather sack. "It's so pretty!" About three inches wide with leather backing, a pattern in colorful glass beads extended the full length of the long strip. Blue, red, green, yellow, and white glistened, a native pattern dancing in the firelight. She held it up to her nose to inhale the scent of fresh leather and ran her fingers over the beads, their slick, rippled effect exciting her. It was the most beautiful thing she'd ever owned.

Her ma grinned. "Your pa bought the beads and leather, Madame provided the leather bag, and your grandmère and I made it in secret while we were at work at Madame's."

"Oui," her maternal grandmother said, tittering. "One day you surprised us with a visit and we had to hide it away."

They helped Cassie wrap it around her thin waist two times, commenting that as she grew, she would eventually wrap it only once. Both ends with leather fringe hung down to her ankles. She hugged all the adults, thrilled to have such gifts and quite certain she was the most blessed girl on the island.

Last to give their gifts, she presented her pictures and maple syrup and her brothers passed out pinecones they'd painted as ornaments for the mantle. They gave Cassie a pinecone, too, even though she'd helped them do the painting.

By the time she snuggled under her quilts, her eyelids felt like lead. As much as she wanted to stay awake to keep thinking about all the wonderful presents she'd received, she drifted off thinking about how lucky she was. "Thank you, Baby Jesus, for being born," she whispered as sleep swept her away to dreamland.

CHAPTER 8

*A*utumn, 2023

"We have a very fat scrapbook." Wanda tapped the top of the leather-bound book with its fancy embossed pattern that would have once been shiny gold. Tarnished and worn, only specks of gold remained but the pattern underneath revealed a Victorian-era flare.

All the items they'd brought down from the trunk in the attic were lined up on the dining room table. There were three things – the scrapbook, something wrapped in dilapidated cloth, and a mottled leather sack the size and heft of a big purse. The wedding dress and its veil hung on a padded hanger. Wanda, James, Alexandra, Madison, and Bernard sat at the table.

Wanda opened the cover of the scrapbook and stopped, hand suspended over a newspaper article. Her pause caused the others to lean in to look.

No one spoke in reverence to what they saw.

Finally, Wanda read the headline:

"TITANIC SINKS FOUR HOURS AFTER HITTING ICEBERG;
866 RESCUED BY CARPATHIA;
PROBABLY 1250 PERISHED...."

Silence ensued again while everyone absorbed the impact of the horrific tragedy.

"*The New York Times,*" Alexandra added as she studied the clipping, "dated Tuesday, April 16, 1912. Does anybody know what day the Titanic sank?"

"It was Monday, April 15th," Bernard offered. "It hit the iceberg late the night before on Sunday the 14th, and it went down four hours later in the wee hours of the morning on the 15th."

Alexandra peered up at her cousin with a glint of awe. "Ah, yes. I suppose an industrial engineer like you would know that."

He nodded solemnly. "That was the hardest part of my job – making sure I never created anything that might harm someone." He'd worked for Ford Motors in Detroit his entire working life, creating systems and machines that would work fluidly with people for efficiency and effectiveness. "I can't imagine the horror the designers of the Titanic felt after its sinking and the loss of so many souls. I would've been traumatized for the rest of my life."

Wanda turned the page of the scrapbook to come upon two more newspaper articles, one on each side of the pages.

New York American shouted:

NO HOPE LEFT

The Boston Daily Globe declared:

ALL DROWNED BUT 868

She shook her head in disbelief as she turned more pages. "Look at this. Page after page of newspaper clippings about the Titanic. I wonder if somebody who lived here knew someone on the ship."

"Maybe not only knew them but was related to them," James added.

Madison said, "I wonder if it was the woman who had the wedding dress. It makes me wonder if she even got a chance to wear it." The others looked at her in surprise, the supposition being so sad. "What if her fiancé was on the ship?"

"Tragedy on top of tragedy," Bernard said, "if that's true. It would explain, though, why she kept the dress and the scrapbook in the same trunk."

Wanda turned to the last page. "Look at this! It says, 'The Marconi International Marine Communication Company, Ltd.' It's a telegram. From the Titanic! Look! It says so right here, 'Office of Origin: Titanic.'" She pointed to the line on the rumpled piece of paper. The stamped lettering was surprising clear. "'Date: April 13, 1912.' The day before it hit the iceberg." She slid the scrapbook over so everyone had a better view. "Imagine!"

"That's incredible." James bent over the book. "The message says, 'To: Ivy Chambers. Home soon, my love. Miss you so. Your Roland.'"

Alexandra took reading glasses out of her pocket to get a better view. "Names. Good. I can do some research on them to see if I can find out what happened here."

"This scrapbook is from the old movie, right? But for real, not the movie." Madison's surprise question hung in the air for the six seconds it took for the older folks to grasp her meaning.

"Yes," Wanda said. "The 'old' movie, which isn't so old to the rest of us, was a dramatized version of this horrible real-life event."

"That was a good movie," Madison innocently said. "Great music. It's so awful that Leonardo DiCaprio drowned. I mean, it's awful that anybody drowned for real."

"Yes, sweet pea, it is." Alexandra gave the teen some slack for her inexperience and naïveté.

"That telegram – in fact this whole book – may well be worth a lot of money if you ever want to sell it to a collector," Bernard suggested. "I'm sure there's a museum somewhere that would love to have this, not to mention private collectors. There are a lot of those. The Titanic is still a big deal."

"Oh, I don't feel like it's ours," James replied. "It belongs to the descendants of Ivy Chambers."

"I agree," Wanda said.

Alexandra nodded assent. "Maybe that name means something to my new client. Her ancestry search has led her to this house. I'll call her this evening and find out."

"Good. Now, we have these other things that were in the trunk, too." Wanda moved over to the lumpy cloth. She carefully opened it to reveal a pile of baby clothes, fragile from age but also from having been well worn. "Handmade baby blue infant and toddler things. Knitted, handsewn ... this one is crocheted."

Madison fingered the clothes, picked up a tiny hat, and held it up. "It's so little." She almost whispered. "So, if she had a baby, she probably did get to wear the wedding dress. She was married." Her voice trailed off and her face fell in sorrow over knowing that wouldn't be the case with her and her baby.

Her Aunt Wanda gave her a quick side hug.

James moved to the third item, a worn leather sack. "And what about this?" He untied the frail ribbon at the top and reached in to bring out a beautifully beaded tie belt. The cracked leather backing made its age apparent, but the colorful glass beads remained bright in a Native American pattern. About three inches wide, its length indicated it would have been tied with plenty left to hang down. He held it up to the light.

"It's beautiful!" Alexandra ran a hand over the beads.

Everyone oooed and aaahed.

James folded it and put it on top of the sack.

Bernard pointed at each thing on the table, one by one. "How incongruous to have a Victorian-era wedding dress, a Titanic scrapbook, baby clothes, and a Native American belt all together."

"How on earth is all of this connected?" Wanda wondered aloud.

The five of them stood there and stared. No one had an answer.

CHAPTER 9

*C*hristmastime, 1837

Each Christmas-day afternoon Chief Joe invited villagers to the Mission House for storytelling time when he'd share a special Odawa tale. The Mission House sat at the edge of the village in a corner of the island. It was the school for Native and Métis children. Even though many were Catholic and the mission was Presbytery, children of both faiths were allowed to attend for the sake of saving their souls. Most pupils lived there, as it was a boarding school, but those from the island remained in their parents' homes. Being Métis herself – a child of a mixed-race mother and a white man – it was where Cassie went to school. Her brothers would eventually go there, too. Or so she thought.

School was a second home to Cassie. She loved the smell of books, the view out the long windows that framed Lake Huron, and the blackboard with its squeaky white chalk. The teacher, the reverend's wife Mrs. Ferry, had written the alphabet in curly letters across the top of the board and Cassie strove to learn to write that pretty, practicing over and over again.

Mrs. Ferry insisted her pupils learn to read, speak, and spell 'proper American.' She didn't like it when they mixed up all the languages they knew. Cassie aimed to please and was very good at 'American.'

She loved to read but the school didn't have many books. She needed more, having repeatedly read everything she could understand from the Bible. She'd also read *The History of Little Henry and his Bearer* six times, the book most kids her age liked. When she grew up, she would buy herself lots of books.

The villagers gathered in the schoolroom, the pupils' benches being taken by women and children and the men standing around the sides. Madame La Framboise was there along with her grown son. Mamo and Grandmère sat with Madame. Even the traveling priest from Ste. Anne's came.

Everyone fell silent when Chief Joe walked in like royalty. Although frightfully old, the chief held himself straight and tall. His long white hair fell in a braid down his back. He wore his fringed leather jacket and Cassie squirmed in her seat to try to get his attention so he could see what she wore, too. She proudly had her Odawa belt tied around her waist atop her coat. He noticed and winked at her, causing her a grin to erupt across her face.

He went to the front of the room and said, "Welcome, my friends. Today I have a story about a belief of my people. I hope you will listen carefully, because it is the most important story I have ever told you. And it is the last."

The crowd gasped. Why would Chief Joe never tell them another story? Was he predicting his own death? Cassie grabbed Ma's hand in fear.

The chief chuckled. "No, I have not had a vision of my own death. But as we can all see ..." he lifted his arms up at his sides and smiled "... that time may not be long off. Do not mourn me when my spirit journeys to the great beyond, as I have lived a good life. I had fifty years with my dear wife." The chief's wife had died the winter before. Many an adult made the sign of the cross over their chest at the mention of the dearly departed. "In fact," the chief continued, "I've had the best life a man could have here on our island. No, I do not plan on dying today." He teased and folks tittered in relief.

"There's another reason this will be my last story. You see, our island is part of Michigan Territory, a part of the United States of America. You know this. What you may not yet know is that after the first of the new year, 1837, it will become a state, an official part of the country."

A rumbling went up in the crowd. Cassie looked around to see some men nodding. They'd known this was coming. Others did not seem pleased. She looked at her pa for guidance. He was so focused on the chief, she couldn't get his attention. Ma patted her knee in reassurance.

"This means," Chief Joe continued, "there will be new laws to follow. That may or may not be a good thing. Time will tell. But one thing we know is that since the fur trade seems to be diminishing, the island has changed."

Feet shuffled as half a dozen grownups jostled around in discomfort. Chief Joe often said the fur trading business would die because white men had no respect for the natural cycle of life, killing too many animals for something other than food and warmth. He'd been saying it for years and they'd ignored him. That was why no fur traders were in the room. They didn't like Chief Joe. Lately, however, they'd found it hard to ignore his warnings as it became harder and harder to find beaver to trap, their primary hide, as the animals' colonies dwindled. They hated to admit the old Indian might be right. He might be highly regarded by many folks on the island but fur traders weren't about to pay him his due.

The chief waited for them to settle down before continuing. "You've heard me tell the story of how the island changed before I was born when French missionaries and fur traders came. For hundreds of years my people had honored the island as a sacred meeting ground where trading amongst tribes took place, and marriages were arranged. That slowly changed when the fur trade came. Soon our island will change again. Fishing is doing well." He motioned toward Pa and Uncle Niall. "Praise God. But what will become of our once-sacred place besides that, we do not know."

He clasped his hands and bowed his head, almost as if in prayer.

No one moved as they waited to him to speak again. It only took seconds but to those waiting, it seemed like an eternity.

"The reason I will no longer be telling stories here is because my son has convinced me to move to the south shore ..." everyone knew he meant the mainland to the south "... to live with him and his family. There's another reason, as well, something I'll let the reverend explain. Then I will tell my final good story at Mission House on Mackinac Island in Michigan Territory."

He nodded at Reverend Ferry, who'd been standing on the side-lines. The rotund preacher strode to the front, solemn as usual, his thumbs crooked into the lapel of his jacket and his starched white collar chafing his neck. He intimidated Cassie and she usually did her best to avoid him.

"My fellow islanders," he said, his voice practically a growl, "as unfortunate as this may be, my family and I will be leaving the island when spring is upon us. The Mission House ..." he motioned around him "... will close. What will become of it, I know not."

A grumble went up from the crowd.

"I know, I know," he went on, gesturing with his palms down to mollify them. "I'm not happy about it either. But we simply cannot afford to keep our mission going. The children will be returned to their homes. Our school and church will close. I pray one of you will step in to make certain island children continue to be properly trained in the ways of our Lord Jesus Christ and in the eyes of God."

Cassie panicked. That meant there wouldn't be any more school.

Madame La Framboise spoke up. "You need not fear, reverend. I will make certain island children have schooling, like I did before you opened your mission here." There was no animosity in her tone. Even though a devout Catholic, she'd always supported the Presbyterian minister's school. A believer in learning, she'd sent her own children to a private school in Montreal to be educated in French culture and Catholicism. Having the mission school, however, had relieved her of the responsibility of teaching other Native and Metís children in her home, which she'd done for several years before the mission school opened.

Cassie relaxed. The thought of going to school at Madame's fine, big house appealed to her. After all, that was where Ma and Grand-mère were every day. She'd see more of them than ever.

"Thank you, Madame," the reverend said to the Odawa matriarch. "That eases my mind. I will continue my ministry, of course, and invite anyone who ventures off the island to visit my new church on the Grand River, any Sunday morning. Now, Chief Joe, it's story time."

Chief Joe returned and spun a yarn that had Cassie sitting on the edge of her seat. She'd heard of this thing he talked about before but never like this. It gave her hope. It inspired her. It could make her dreams come true.

CHAPTER 10

*A*utumn, 2023

"Aunt Wanda, tell me the story of our ancestors who lived here on the island."

Wanda and Madison sat by the fireplace in the living room, Madison with her legs tucked under her on the sofa and Wanda stretched out in a chair with her feet on an ottoman. Each had a knitted afghan thrown over her. After Alexandra and Bernard left, it turned chilly and started raining again. So James chivalrously built a fire then went to work in his study, leaving the girls to chat.

"I sent a family tree to your mom," Wanda said. "Did she show it to you?"

"No. I never knew she got one. But she did complain that you kept wanting to tell her about a bunch of dead people in our family."

"Pfft. Of course she did. I'll show it to you later. Having the illustration helps, but here's the nitty gritty, although there's much more to tell. But let me ask you something first," Wanda said as Madison cocked her head in quandary. "Why do you want to know?"

The teen looked at the fire in thought for a few moments then with an intense gaze came back to her aunt. "I don't know. It just interests me. I mean, all those people. We wouldn't be here without them. Right?"

"Right. They went through a lot to get us here. I believe we need to appreciate them."

"Yeah, that makes sense."

"Plus, you're having a baby, Madison. That's a marvelous thing, as much as it doesn't seem like it right now. Knowing your heritage puts life into perspective for your future and for the future of your child. It gives us gratitude and humbles us when we know about the sacrifices our forebears made to keep their families going, families that resulted in us."

"Wow. That's a lot."

Wanda threw her head back and chuckled. "Okay, okay. I got a little preachy. But you get my drift, don't you?"

"Sure. I get it. I need to be grateful to all the people who made me and my baby."

"That's it. First, let me tell you a bit about the island. I promise not to lecture. But it's fascinating. Think about this: there were many branches of Odawa and other native tribes that met on the island in the summertime for centuries. They spoke a variety of native languages but managed to trade goods and food. They even arranged marriages."

"Geez. I wish they could help me out with that so my baby would have a daddy."

"Your baby will have a wonderful mother."

"Yeah, whether it's me or somebody I pick to adopt it. But go on about the dead people."

"Wait. You're thinking of putting your baby up for adoption? I'm not judging, mind you, just curious."

"I don't …" the teen's voice faltered "… I don't really want to. But I don't have a choice. Do I? I mean, I wanna finish school and go to college and have a career and get married someday. How can I do all that with a child to take care of? I don't know how to take care of a baby. But then I think about having it …" she placed a protective hand on her belly "… and handing it over to strangers and never seeing it again. It's like … like my heart bleeds."

Wanda studied her young niece, so innocent yet so pregnant. The girl was facing one of the most difficult challenges women throughout the ages had faced. "How about we take some time to make that decision? You don't have to decide at this moment. You don't have to know everything right now. I'll help you make the decision within the next couple of months, by the time the baby comes. How's that?"

Madison's features relaxed. Her eyes brightened. She exhaled a long breath of relief. "Okay. That sounds good. Thank you, Aunt Wanda."

"There's something you need to know, sweetie. James is very rich. He's already told me we can support you in any way necessary."

"I, well, I, um, I don't think that's right. I mean, ah …"

"Don't decide anything about that right now, either. Take your time. We'll figure out everything together. Tell me, before you got pregnant, what did you foresee for your future?"

"Besides marrying Gavin?"

"Oh, yes. Before Gavin."

"Well, I've never told anybody 'cuz it sounds crazy."

"Crazy works in this house."

"Ever since I was a little kid, I've wanted to be an ambulance driver. I wanna be the EMT that saves lives, too, but I especially wanna drive the truck. I used to watch TV shows that had ambulances, you know, like *Gray's Anatomy*, and that's what I wanted to do."

"That's very admirable. I suspect that in order to be the driver, you have to be an EMT for a while and get promoted to driving. I'm not sure about that, but it sounds plausible."

"Oh that's fine. I would love to do that. When I was little, I had a nurse's kit and liked pretending I was making people better when they were sick."

"We can research what kind of training is required for that job. First, of course, you'll need to finish high school. Do you think you'll want to go back or do it online?"

"Online. I'm never going back."

"Do you miss it? Your friends, classes you liked …. You were a cheerleader, right? Do you miss any of it?"

"Yeah, sorta. But most of my friends got so snarky when I got pregnant, I realized they weren't really my friends."

"Ah, yes. That's how that works, I'm afraid."

"Yeah, it does. Hey," Madison said, abruptly changing the subject, "Tell me more about the Native women. That'll make me feel better. Like you said, they had it a lot harder than me."

"I'm sure they did. Harder than me, too."

Wanda fell into the past, her mind traveling back in time to experience what it had been like for her many-times great-grandmothers Gichigama and Gichigama's daughter Cassandra. She and Alexandra had been able to dig up quite a few facts in census and church records but without a journal or diary or letters, she'd never know exactly what those women's lives were like. Based on her research of the island, however, she could make some educated guesses.

"I'll start with what life was like on the island. I like to think about it from the natives' perspective," she began. "It's a time before Europeans arrive. Natives revere this island as sacred. As I mentioned, a variety of tribes gather here in the summertime to trade goods, celebrate, and arrange marriages. It's against their beliefs to marry within a clan that's made up mostly of extended family. So marrying into another clan is common. The shores of the island are lined with huts and teepees. Summer is an exciting, peaceful time, something to look forward to throughout the long winter." She took a sip of the coffee that sat at her side.

"It sounds wonderful," Madison said. "I love camping. I would've liked it."

"Me, too. Then, however, in the 1600s, these strange people with white skin who dress funny and speak an unintelligible language show up out of nowhere. First French fur traders come, rugged men who speak that weird language. Then men the natives call 'Black Robes' arrive. They call them that because of their clothes. It turns out they're Catholic missionary priests who want them to change their traditional spiritual beliefs. The priests are followed by many more

French fur traders. So, the natives learn to speak French. Now they know five or six languages, including the variety of native tongues and French."

"I could hardly pass Spanish I."

"Yeah, they had to be smart, right? Then more people show up. English. Americans. Irish and Scots. A few Germans and Poles. You get the idea. And you know what?"

Madison shook her head.

"Many of the natives learn more languages and figure out how to get along with everybody. And they're called savages. Huh! They're brilliant. Many French fur traders marry native women for the sake of solidifying business arrangements in the fur trade. We can only hope some of those marriages are happy. Women from other countries join their men and have children who grow up and marry into cultures other than their own. The island is one great big mixture of different types of human beings."

"Wow. I never thought about all that. I like how you tell it like it's happening now. I can imagine it. You're a good storyteller, Aunt Wanda."

"Thank you, sweetie. I tell you all of this because that's the world our ancestors lived in. They somehow, miraculously, survived all those changes. And here we are. They made it and we will, too. You will."

"I know. I guess I believe that. It's just so hard. Tell me more about the first ancestor you know about. That woman named Gichi-something."

Wanda went on to tell the story of Gichigama Geneviève St. Croix McIntyre, known as Gichi, and her daughter Cassandra Colleen. At least, she told as much as she knew.

Madison listened intently and asked a few questions, then stretched out on the sofa and fell asleep. Wanda quietly put a log on the fire and went to check on her hubby in his study.

James invited her to sit on his lap, where he proceeded to shower her with kisses. This was the kind of bliss Wanda had always craved. An imaginary picture of Gichi flitted across her mind. Her ancestor had lived a rough life on the American frontier and here Wanda was with everything any woman could ever want.

"You know what, honey?" She kissed her husband's forehead.

"Dare I venture a guess?"

"You'll never guess this. I've been telling Madison about our ancestors and it just occurred to me that they'd be thrilled to see me so happy and so blessed. It makes me want to enjoy and appreciate what I have – that's you, my love. It makes me want to enjoy you all the more. It would be an insult to them if I didn't."

"Well, then, I have an idea about how we can be the happiest any couple could possibly ever be. To make sure we don't insult your ancestors, of course."

She grinned like a minx. "And what, pray tell, might that be?"

"Follow me and I promise you won't be disappointed." He slid her off his lap, stood up, and took her hand. "Come with me, my bride."

Quietly, so as not to wake their guest, they tiptoed up the stairs to their room, closed the door, and proceeded to become the happiest couple on earth.

CHAPTER 11

Christmastime, 1837

Everyone in Mission House settled in as Chief Joe began his story. Whispering ceased; a barn owl hooted outside; and the scraping of only one man's boots against the wood floor could be heard as the fellow found a spot where he could lean against the wall.

"Many suns and moons ago," the chief began, "the first people, my ancestors, believed this island to be sacred. It was therefore a perfect place to come to for pimadaziwin. Now I know that is a hard word for white people to say. Say it with me in pieces."

No one knew for sure how old Chief Joe might be, although Cassie had heard grownups say he must be near a hundred. His crystal brown eyes and pure white teeth looked young. His dark skin, however, with its crinkles going in every direction like chicken scratches in the dirt, appeared to be ancient. Yet she'd known old people before who didn't stand up straight and didn't have strong voices. He must be, she decided, about seventy. It wasn't all the way to a hundred but, still, it was awfully old.

"Pima," he said.

The crowd repeated the sound.

"Dazi."

The sound rang out in a chorus of voices.

"Win!"

Folks clapped and yelled, "Win!"

"Pimadaziwin!"

Everyone joined in and playfully repeated the long Odawa word.

"It means being given the blessing of a good life, a gift to live long and free of illness and misfortune." He paused, scanning his audience with intensity. "But how does a person obtain this blessing?" Blank, anxious stares answered. "This gift is granted by dream visitors who have the power to overcome adversity."

Cassie flinched when he shouted "power," drilling that word into her mind and, no doubt, the minds of everyone within earshot. But how did a person find these dream visitors to get power? Her squirming in her seat caused her ma to put an arm around her shoulder to settle her down.

"But, my friends," the chief continued, gesturing broadly as he spoke, "dream visitors do not grant this power to everyone. People who are inhospitable, stingy, greedy, and who ridicule others – they will never be granted this gift. An immoral man or woman will be shunned by the dream visitors. For you see, they only want for those who are considerate of one another and care about the earth to live long and well. The blessing will be granted to those who gaze at the sky and think about how they must live so that seven generations after them can also live well. They will be good stewards of the earth so that the next seven generations may live on this beautiful land as they did. They will not be selfish with the abundances they have found here."

Cassie glanced around the room to find Ian standing by his da. Her cousin's eyes were homed in on Chief Joe. The way Ian stood at attention, the way his face was so alert, it was as if the lad was experiencing some kind of revelation. And then she knew. The chief was telling white people they were not paying attention to the ways of the Indians, and that would be to their peril. She didn't understand the details, but somehow she knew this was a lesson in life that would make sense someday.

The chief's voice softened. "Where might you find these dream visitors? Well, clearly, you must be dreaming for them to come." Titters rippled throughout the crowd. "But you need not be asleep, necessarily, although you can do that, too. You must first find a place that you find sacred. Never mind if it is a special place to anyone else. It can be your own bed or it can be outdoors. It can be sitting by the fire in the evening. It can be standing on the shore looking out over the lake. It can be in a canoe gliding over the water. It can be the cave in the middle of the island."

Cassie blinked. The cave was her special place. Chief Joe must be a mind-reader to know that, as she'd always kept it a secret. He smiled at her.

"You must be in this place of solitude by yourself or at least undisturbed by others. And you must open your mind and your heart and your very soul ..." his voice became deeper and deeper until it rumbled "... to beseech the dream visitors to come to you with this blessing of a long, fulfilling life." His face relaxed and his voice brightened. "You must tell them you know you are worthy, for you are good to people, to animals, to the earth, and best of all to yourself." He emphasized yourself, making it two words, *your self.* "You must not lie when you say this, for they will know and you will never be blessed. Only when they know you tell the truth will they bestow this gift upon you."

Cassie panicked and racked her brain to try to remember how many white lies she'd told in her life. The time she told Ma she hadn't eaten the last apple flashed across her mind. She made a quick vow to never lie again.

The chief paced back and forth across the front of the room, pointing at people as he went. "Now, you might be wondering, 'Who are these dream visitors?' Remember that I told you to respect the seven generations after you?" Heads nodded throughout the room. "The dream visitors are the seven generations who came before you. They are those who honored you before you were born, so that they would leave you the legacy of a good life. They are your ancestors. We honor those who came before and those who will come after. That is what gives us a good life."

He almost whispered his final words, leaving his rapt audience leaning forward to capture his final missive. Without any hubbub, he nodded, marched to the door, opened it, and closed it gently behind him as he went out into the wintery afternoon.

No one spoke for long moments until one man said, "Well! That was interesting. Sorry the old fellow won't be with us anymore."

Cassie realized the man hadn't understood the chief's story. He didn't know it was real. The crowd became jovial for the most part, although some remained solemn, lost is thought.

Ian came over to Cassie and said, "I'm gonna miss Chief Joe."

"Yeah, me, too."

"Let's go visit him before he goes away."

"Sure. When?"

"Now."

She told Ma where she was going and they started down the lane toward town where the chief lived in a hut. But as they passed Madame's grand house, they saw him go around the side toward the backdoor. They followed and watched as he entered the kitchen. When they got there, the door stood ajar. Ian pushed it open.

Chief Joe said, "Come in, my friends." They went in and Ian made sure the door closed tight against the winter chill. "Take off your coats and hang them up," the chief said as he motioned toward the pegs by the door where his jacket hung.

Ian helped Cassie unwrap her belt so she could take off her coat and hang it up. Protectively, she hung the belt over it.

The old man glanced back at them as he fed wood into the vast fireplace. Madame would have let the fire die down while she was gone. No workers were in the house seeing that it was a holy day. The fire flared and Chief Joe motioned for the youngsters to sit on the stools nearby while he sat in a cushioned chair next to the fire. He took his pipe out of the pocket of his plaid flannel shirt and lit it with a splinter of wood he stuck in the flames.

It occurred to Cassie that he and Madame must be very good

friends, as he was so comfortable in her home even though she wasn't there. Just then, Madame came in with a cheerful hello and wishes for a merry Christmas as she hung her wrap and hat on a peg.

"Ah, Cassie," she said, "I see you wore your Odawa belt today." She ran her aging hand over the beads. "I am pleased that you honor it so." She joined them in a second chair by the fire.

"Yes, Madame." The girl wasn't sure what kind of response was called for but agreeing seemed safe enough.

"Your ancestors are pleased," the chief informed her.

That relieved Cassie, as she'd been a bit concerned about the lying thing. "Chief Joe, where do the dream visitors live?" she wanted to know.

He and Madame exchanged a knowing glance, and he said, "They live everywhere, dear child. They live in the woods and the water and the sky and, best of all, they live in your soul. They are already within you, waiting to be found."

Cassie clapped a hand to her chest. "They're inside me?"

"Yes, little one. You already have what you need to live a full and abundant life. You simply need to pay attention to the wisdom your ancestors have passed down within you and open your heart to let them guide you."

"Chief Joe," Ian interjected, "I think I feel them inside me. I think they talk to me."

This was a shocking revelation to Cassie. No one inside her ever talked to her. She'd never heard Ian mention this and feared either he was lying to please the grownups or he had a whole world he'd never shared with her. She felt left out.

"What do they say?" Madame wanted to know.

Ian tossed a quick glance at Cassie as if afraid to let the cat out of the bag lest she share it with their family. This was a big secret indeed. But he let it out anyway. "I want to go on adventures. I've heard fur traders tell stories about pirates on the ocean sea who steal and plunder. And a hero named Robin Hood. I want to be like Robin Hood and go on grand adventures across the sea. I will take back what the pirates stole and give it to the poor."

Cassie was no fool. She'd heard those stories, too, mostly from Pa. But she couldn't imagine going off to the big ocean sea. She couldn't imagine ever leaving her island.

Chief Joe and Madame La Framboise nodded approval of Ian's admission. Cassie found herself shaking her head no.

"You must keep that desire in your heart, young Ian." The chief pointed with his pipe. "You must never let it be forgotten. It may change in some ways as you grow older, but the essence of it will live within you forever. You'll find, like we have …" he gestured toward Madame "… that no matter what happens, no matter how many changes come into your life, even those that are uninvited, you have the power to love being alive here on Earth."

Ian said, "Thank you, Chief Joe."

The chief's eye glinted in the firelight as he puffed on his pipe, the smoke circling his face, giving him an otherworldly aura. Cassie found her old friend to be quite magical but confusing at the same time. She didn't know what to make of all this talk but knew she'd never forget it.

The children left Madame's house with Ian happily trotting toward home. Cassie trudged along behind him. When they'd almost reached their houses, he turned and hollered, "Hey! Wanna go sledding?"

She smiled and ran to him. "Let's go!"

Thank goodness, her Ian was back.

CHAPTER 12

*a*utumn, 2023

When Barb Rand walked into Wanda's cottage, the wedding dress and veil hanging in the dining room immediately caught her eye. "It's so beautiful!" she marveled. "I'm quite certain this was my grandmother's." She lovingly fingered two long, white, linen dresses from the same era that hung beside it.

"I found the wedding dress first," Wanda explained, "and we've found more since."

Barb turned to the table with its attic finds. She opened the Titanic scrapbook and tears welled in her eyes. Wanda, Alexandra, and Madison remained silent out of respect as she took off her glasses and found a tissue in her purse to wipe her face. "Oh my, this is so moving." She sat down, so they all sat down and watched as she turned the pages and read the articles. When she closed the book, she said, "I have letters that will explain all of this."

"We can't wait to read them," Alexandra replied.

"They are unbelievably moving. I didn't ever expect this, to see what's described in the letters. I want to see the house, though, if you don't mind, before we get to those. This is where my grandmother lived." She looked around, agog with wonder.

Barb stood – so everyone stood – and moved on to the baby clothes. "Oh, how precious." The beaded Native belt gave her pause and then she said, "My letters tell us who this came from."

Delighted to hear that after a week of waiting and wondering, the other three became riveted to the tote bag that Barb had sitting on an empty chair at the dining room table. The past week of champing at the bit to learn more about their attic find would've been more nerve-racking if they hadn't been so busy. Their days had been jam-packed with activity. Wanda and Alexandra took Madison to the clinic for an exam and the doctor declared her "hale and hearty." There was no equipment there to determine the gender of the baby, so that remained a mystery. They took the ferry to St. Ignace in the upper peninsula and bought clothes that fit the mom-to-be and lots of baby supplies. They'd also gone through more trunks in the attic and found more clothes. James spent the week hustling around to get ready for his trip to Antarctica. He'd left the day before to a flurry of goodbyes.

And, finally, Barb Rand, Alexandra's genealogy client who had a connection to the cottage, arrived on a gloriously sunny and colorful day, the autumn leaves at their peak and flowers in full bloom. The three islanders walked down the long hill from the West Bluff to the dock to greet their visitor upon her arrival. The older women had insisted Madison stay home but she wouldn't hear of it. The brisk walk on such a beautiful day invigorated them and they were in a frolicking mood by the time they reached the dock.

The Shepler's ferry pulled up to the dock, only about three-quarters full, unlike being stuffed to the gills at the height of the summer season. Several people got off with their dogs, some with bicycles, and a few with backpacks. There were no families, as school was in session. Toward the end, however, Wanda was delighted to see a bride in her white wedding dress and veil, which fluttered in the gentle breeze as she and her two bridesmaids disembarked. She wished the bride well as the cheerful wedding party bounded away.

She quickly realized, however, she'd been a bit insensitive. Madison had turned away. There was no wedding in the teen's future, even though she was large with child.

The last person off the ferry was their Barb Rand. A robust woman of about seventy with short white hair, bright brown eyes, and smooth tawny skin, her broad smile lifted the mood again. She carried a humungous purse and a tote bag. "Hello there!" she shouted, her arms raised in a vivacious greeting.

After warm hellos all around, they collected her larger bag from the dock porter, and Alexandra hailed a carriage taxi for the ride up the hill to the cottage. As usual for newcomers to the island, as they rode by Barb marveled at the charm of the village, the loveliness of the cottage homes, and the opulence of the Grand Hotel.

"You will love what I have to show you," Barb said along the way, the cadenced clip-clop of horses hoofs a backdrop to her conversation. "It's all right here." She patted her tote bag. "When my grandmother died years ago, these letters went to her oldest daughter, my aunt. Well, Aunt Tullie didn't give a hoot about a bunch of old letters and stuffed them away. When she died recently, her daughter, my cousin, got them. But thank the Lord above, she had enough decency to ask me if I wanted them before she tossed them out. I know they have value. Not only for our family but for history, as well. You'll see."

It had already been decided that Barb would stay at Wanda's considering that Alexandra's house was small. The big cottage had six bedrooms and five bathrooms. Barb had been searching for an inexpensive inn, as her funds were limited, so the cottage once owned by her ancestors simply made sense.

Once inside, even before Wanda could escort their guest upstairs to her room, Barb had spied the items in the dining room. After looking at that and a cursory tour of the house, Barb announced she needed to rest.

Wanda took her upstairs and got her settled in, then came back downstairs to find the place empty. On the front porch she found her friend and her niece both sound asleep. Madison was curled up on the swing and Alexandra slept with her head back on her cushioned chair and her feet up on the matching ottoman. Wanda went back inside, got two throws, and went out to gently cover them up. It wasn't a cold day but being fall, it wasn't altogether warm, either.

She sat down in the remaining chair and looked out across the colorful trees decked out in their autumn best. She swore she could always breathe better in fall air but suspected it might be the lush beauty that made her think so. Beyond the trees Lake Huron stretched for miles, butting up to the Mackinac Bridge, beyond which was Lake Michigan. The Great Lakes region truly was one of the most beautiful places on earth.

Her mind wandered back to a time-gone-by when her ancestors lived on the island. She wondered about her five-times great-grandmother's, Gichi's, girlhood and if she'd anticipated marrying a Frenchman someday. She also wondered about Cassandra and what her life might have been like. As a child, did she have dreams and aspirations? What did she look forward to in adulthood? Did she look forward to anything at all?

Her head lolled back onto the pillow as she considered that era and the dramatic changes that took place. How well had her forebears coped? Had change crushed their way of life? She dozed as hazy images of the past drifted through her sleepy head.

CHAPTER 13

*N*ew Year's Day, 1838

Cassie couldn't believe what she was hearing. All the grownups sounded so happy! How could they? Had they lost their minds? This was devastating news.

Ian was going away.

They were having a new year celebration at Uncle Liam and Aunt Saoirse's house when Uncle Liam made the announcement. Both McIntyre families crowded around the table for a pork roast dinner. Ian sat there grinning like he thought he was some kind of prince or something.

Cassie despised him for it.

All the younger kids seemed as confused as she was but they didn't dare say anything, either. The grownups had spoken and that was that.

She'd had enough! She pulled her legs up to her chest, spun around on the bench she shared with the other kids, and dashed away from the table. This time she remembered to shuck her shoes and stick her feet in her boots and grab her coat and hat. Her ma and pa called out to her but she ignored them as she yanked open the door and slammed it shut behind her as hard as she could. She threw on her coat and hat, got her mittens out of her pockets, and put them on as she ran down the road away from town.

A layer of light snow rendered her pure white by the time she arrived at her small cave in the middle of the island. Huddled inside, she felt safe from the outside world. Strange things were happening out there.

She closed her eyes, wishing she'd grabbed a piece of Mamo's blackberry cake. It'd been sitting right there on a plate, waiting for dessert time. Her mouth watered. She dozed but the tempting smell of cake woke her up. For a second she thought she was dreaming but when her eyes focused, there it was right in front of her face.

"Go ahead, take it." Ian held it out to her.

He sat beside her, all bundled up in his winter wear. He'd gone through the trouble to wrap the cake in a clean cloth, which hung down over his gloved hand to expose the treat. Cassie hesitated. Ian had become the enemy. Should she accept such an offering from a foe?

She tore off her gloves, grabbed the cake, and took a bite.

"Cassie," he said, "I know you like me, even though you pretend you don't."

"No, I don't. I hate you."

He had the gull to grin. "Well, I don't hate you. I think we're friends. You like sledding with me, don't you?"

She didn't respond as she chewed on her cake.

"Anyway, I'm happy to be going away to school in Montreal. Madame La Framboise is awfully nice to pay for it."

Cassie swallowed and said, "But why do you want to go away?"

"Well, you know how I like school a lot. Come spring we won't even have a school. I like to read all kinds of books. More than the Bible. You and me and most of the people here speak lots of languages. Why, we can talk Irish and English and French and Odawa. Oui, ikwezens colleen?"

A grin escaped at the flattery. He'd said, "Yes, pretty girl," in French, Odawa, and Irish.

"Did you know most people around the world can't do that?" he asked.

She shook her head, her eyes wide in disbelief.

"So in some ways, we're special. That's what Madame told me when she asked me if I wanted to go to school in Montreal. She even said our teacher Mrs. Ferry told her I'm special 'cuz I always know the answers and I'm good at arithmetic. Aw, shucks, I don't think that's so special. You know lots of answers, too."

Her head popped up in pride as she swallowed the last bite of her cake.

"Anyway, I wanna go." Ian reached out to her but let his hand drop. "I wanna take a boat all the way there and see new places and read a whole bunch of books. Madame says they have lots and lots of books at that school. She said they play a game there, too, one they learned from the natives where they hit a ball with sticks. That sounds like fun. After going to that school, when I grow up, I'll be smart and can do whatever I want."

"But ... but don't you wanna be a fisherman like our pa's?"

"Nah. I'm don't much like fish. And I sure don't wanna be a boxer like them."

He pretended to punch her with an upper cut but stopped short. She couldn't help but notice the small scar under his chin where she'd once decked him.

"I'm sorry I hit you, Ian." It was the first time she'd ever apologized but it seemed the prudent thing to do. Maybe he'd stay if he knew she was sorry.

"Aw, shucks, that's okay. It didn't hurt none. Not much, anyway."

"You're not really going away, are you?"

"Yeah, I am. I'll be going on an adventure, Cassie. It's my pimadazi-win, like Chief Joe said. My ancestors want me to go out into the world and discover new things. So you won't be mad at me, will you?"

Her heart sank. Ian was such a pest. But he'd always been her pest. Who would she play with? Who would tease her? Who would she go sledding with?

"Listen, I don't go until after school is out in the spring," he noted. "Let's have a good ol' time until then. Wanna go sledding?"

She brightened. "Sure."

They got up and left Cassie's Cave. On the way back into town, Ian said, "When I leave, Cassie, you can have my sled."

That lifted her mood considerably. She would do as her cousin suggested – have fun for now and put the rest out of her mind.

She found it best to not think about it at all.

CHAPTER 14

*A*utumn, 2023

After a good rest and a mid-afternoon snack of cookies and cantaloupe, they gathered around one end they'd cleared at the dining room table. Barb opened her treasure bag and brought out a large white envelope.

"Let me tell you about this first," she began, her hands gently placed atop the envelope as if it were holy. "There are three letters here. They're what led me to this house. As you'll see, the return address on each envelope is this very cottage. They were written by my grandmother, who lived here, to her sister."

"Once I had names," Alexandra explained to Wanda and Madison, "I was able to confirm these relationships through census and birth records."

"Yes," Barb said, "that's been so helpful. I've read the letters over and over and I'm telling you, we'd better have the tissues ready." She looked around for a box.

"Here." Wanda got up, went into the kitchen, and came back with a fat box of Kleenex. "This should do it." She placed it in the center of the table.

"Okay, here they are." Barb took out three aged letters, handling them as delicately as rose pedals off the flower. "How about this? I can read the first one out loud, then you can take turns reading the other two."

"Did you used to be a teacher?" Madison asked.

Barb guffawed with pleasure. "It shows, huh?"

"Yeah. You sound like a teacher. You know, organized and all." Madison grinned at her. "You sound like my social studies teacher. I loved her."

"Aw, as a former teacher of history for thirty years, I'm glad to hear that."

Wanda was fully aware of the fact that Barb hadn't asked about or commented on Madison's pregnancy. Probably nothing shocked her, Wanda realized, after having been around teens for three decades.

All eyes homed in on the small stack of letters, tied together with a yellow satin ribbon. She slid the top letter out of the ribbon and showed them the return address on the envelope, which was indeed this very cottage.

"Look at that. Beautiful cursive writing. And this." Alexandra pointed at the little red stamp. "George Washington and it cost two cents. My oh my, times have changed."

"It's dated December 26, 1911." It was Wanda's turn to point.

"Just a few months before the Titanic," Madison noticed.

"Yes, and thus it's a very happy letter indeed." Barb opened the envelope, took out the two-page letter, and unfolded it to reveal more florid writing. She read aloud.

December 26, 1911

Dear Anne,

Yesterday was the happiest day of my life. Roland and I are now wed. As you know, the ceremony was held at the Little Stone Church here on the island. Oh, Anne, my sweet sister, it was so very lovely. My gown

THE PROMISE OF CHRISTMAS PRESENT

is so pretty and our grandmother's veil that you gave me was the perfect final touch. Knowing that grandmother, mother, and you all wore it at your weddings made it even more special.

They all looked back at the gown hanging on the mirror. Barb got up and held out the veil to reveal its intricate lace pattern. "Just think, my great-great-grandmother, great-grandmother, and grandmother wore this. I would've loved to wear it, had I known it existed." She sat back down and continued reading.

I so wish you could have been here to witness it but staying in for the sake of your child who is due to be born at any moment was certainly the wise thing to do. Travel would not have been advisable. I look forward to meeting our new family member as soon as we return from our honeymoon and cannot wait to hold the infant in my arms to become an auntie.

For our honeymoon, we are taking the train to New York City where we'll embark upon a journey across the Atlantic to tour Europe. "The continent," I believe is the hoity-toity way to say it. Of course, I've never been out of the state of Michigan, so I await with bated breath to see Italy, Germany, France, and England. After three months we will come home on the maiden voyage of the Titanic, the ship that is supposedly unsinkable. I certainly hope so.

It is on our train trip home that Roland and I expect to stop in Detroit to see you and your burgeoning family.

My adoring love to you all,
Your happily married sister,
Ivy

No one spoke. The ramifications of this message were clear. Newlyweds were on the Titanic. What a horrifying experience. The bride, at least, survived, because she went on to have children, one of whom was Barb's grandfather.

"Did her groom, this Roland, survive?" Wanda wanted to know.

"That's a story unto itself," Barb rasped, her voice rough from holding back tears. She grabbed a tissue and dabbed at the corners of her eyes. "It's in the next letter."

"Hello! Anybody home?" Bernard hollered from the back door.

"In the dining room," Wanda let him know.

His heavy footfall on the wood floors tracked him as he came into the room. "Hello everybody …" He faltered upon seeing Barb.

Wanda introduced the two and they all chatted for a bit. It wasn't long, however, before Wanda realized that her seventy-five-year-old neighbor Bernard was smitten with her seventy-year-old guest Barb. Totally, utterly, schoolboy smitten. She suggested they take a break from reading the letters and invited Alexandra and Madison into the kitchen to help her "do something." Considering there was nothing for them to do, they peeked into the dining room to discover two white-haired heads bowed toward one another, lost in deep discussion.

"What are they talking about?" Madison whispered.

"She's probably explaining the letters," Wanda offered.

"Nah. He's my cousin. I know him. He's asking her out." Alexandra snickered.

"Wow. He works fast," Madison marveled.

"Honey," Alexandra said, "at his age, he can't waste time."

CHAPTER 15

Summertime, 1847

"Cassie, love, here comes another one."

Uncle Niall pointed out the window of his pub, where the Polish man who'd come to town a few months earlier, Krzysztof Kozlowski, approached with flowers in hand. The Pole was so perfectly tall, musclebound, and handsome that Cassie found it difficult to lay eyes on him.

"You'd better get a move on," Aunt Saoirse advised. "He's so big it only takes him two strides to cross the street."

"Ugh," Cassie groaned. "Tell him I'm not here." She dashed to the back door and slid outside.

Niall's Pub was a new log building on the edge of town. Her uncle had tired of the fishing business and refused to get his "noggin lobbed off" anymore by boxing. He and his wife opened the pub a year earlier and had enjoyed a booming business ever since. He'd invited his brother Liam to join them but Cassie's pa said he couldn't imagine being stuck indoors all day every day when they lived in God's most beautiful country. He liked fishing. And boxing.

Cassie, now seventeen years old, worked in the pub a few hours a day. She didn't like being inside, either, but Uncle Niall paid her twenty-five cents a week. She was frugal with her earnings and had ten dollars saved. She didn't have plans yet for spending it but felt grownup having cash stashed away under her mattress.

She had her own small bed now with a real mattress and shared the bedroom with Mamo. The adults in the house had all agreed that, now that she'd blossomed into a young woman, Cassie needed privacy from her younger brothers. She was ever so grateful, as hiding her burgeoning breasts had become difficult, especially with them being curious boys.

Now the problem was that men kept staring at those breasts and falling in love with her. Krzysztof was a nice enough fellow but she found him, well, dull. He didn't read books. She couldn't imagine spending her life with someone who didn't like to read.

She stood outside with her ear pressed to the backdoor of the pub. The voices were muffled but she heard Uncle Niall say, "Ack, I'm sorry Krzysztof. Cassie isna here. Can I get ya a pint?"

Cassie relaxed. The Pole loved his ale. He'd be in there for a good while.

Then she heard Aunt Saoirse say, "Why, thank you so much for the flowers. I'll put them in a vase on the shelf behind the bar where everyone can see them."

Cassie snickered. Her aunt had saved him embarrassment over the flowers.

She took off her apron, hung it on a nail outside by the door, skirted the side of the building so she wouldn't be seen through the window, and headed for home. It was a gorgeous spring day and she wanted to take a nice, long ride on her horse, Doodles.

Her parents had somehow managed to purchase the gray mare when she was nine, a gift to mollify her over her despair that her best friend and cousin, Ian, was gone. She loved riding and had become an excellent horsewoman. She and Doodles could handle a dray with the best of them, too. In fact, it was Cassie who drove the dray from the dock to the pub when supplies of ale and whiskey arrived by boat. Doodles could do it all and had become Cassie's best friend.

She'd only walked a short way, her mind on where she and

Doodles would ride to that day, when heavy footsteps approached from behind. She spun around to find the giant barreling toward her, felt hat in hand, held over his chest.

"Miss Cassie! May I walk you home?" The Pole's stilted accent masked a gentle voice.

"Um, I guess," she acquiesced. They started out toward her house. "Put your hat back on, Krzysztof," she said. "You don't have to be formal with me." He did as instructed. She glanced over at him and, quite suddenly, a realization came to her. She stopped and faced him. His cheeks blushed in anticipation. "Krzysztof, do you know *how* to read?"

His rosy cheeks turned white with shame. "I confess, Miss Cassie, that I cannot do."

"Would you like to learn?"

"Oh, tak. I mean yes. I would like to learn to read more than anything. But I am too old. That is for children."

They strolled on again.

"How old are you?" she asked. She knew he was considerably older than she, as he'd been a shanty man, someone who felled trees, before coming to the island. Now he helped build the new places going up around the village. He even helped build Niall's Pub.

"I am afeared that if I say, you will find me unfitting."

"How old?" she insisted.

He bowed his head and spoke into his chest. "Thirty-five."

That was quite old, she conceded, but she had enough couth to refrain from saying it. An idea struck and she stopped him again. "Have you met the new teacher in town? Miss Abby?"

"I have seen her from afar."

"Let's go meet her now."

"But why, Miss Cassie? I am courting you."

"Nah. You don't want me." She waved a hand of dismissal. "Miss Abby is thirty, I would say, and she's very pretty. And I'd bet my eye teeth she'd love to teach you to read. You're not too old, Krzysztof. Not too old at all."

"Are you sure, Miss Cassie? Might she find me unpleasing?"

She eyed him up and down. Most women would grovel at the feet of a manly specimen like him. "Oh, trust me, she will find you very pleasing. Come on. Let's go." She hurried along until they reached the boarding house where the teacher lived.

It only took fifteen minutes before the Pole and the teacher forgot that Cassie McIntyre so much as existed. She tip-toed off the porch and left them laughing together on the swing. That had gone even better than she'd hoped. Usually, she wasn't so lucky.

There had been the private from the post when she was fifteen. He'd been mad as a hatter when she refused his proposal of marriage out of hand.

A new young preacher in town had proposed, as well, but she found him far too stodgy. He found another parish in Ohio and left shortly thereafter.

The rich fellow who worked for the American Fur Company had seemed nice enough at first but as she got to know him, he seemed conceited. He even wanted her to move to New York City with him. She couldn't imagine such a thing. When she mentioned that to him, as well as the fact he seemed a tad conceited, he bellowed that he'd intended to propose but would have nothing to do with a half-breed who worked in a pub. She didn't bother to inform him she was a quarter-breed. He was out. Pa proclaimed him "an arsehole."

Still, her parents were befuddled that their beautiful daughter couldn't manage to get herself married, like most girls her age. But they never rebuked her about it, thankfully, instead having apparently given up on the notion that she would ever find an acceptable mate.

And that suited Cassie just fine. She saddled up Doodles and rode like the wind around the shore of the island. Never would she let any man take her freedom away from her. And never would she settle for anything less than what she wanted.

CHAPTER 16

*A*utumn, 2023

After the new later-in-life lovebirds, Barb and Bernard, had fifteen minutes to "chirpsong," as Madison called it, Wanda, Alexandra, and Madison returned to the dining room to rejoin them.

"Barb's been explaining these letters to me," Bernard told them. "How fascinating."

"Yeah, I bet." Alexandra's covert tease went unnoticed by the smitten ones but Wanda and Madison got it.

Everyone took a seat. Alexandra volunteered to read the next letter.

Barb became grim, her hand shaking as she took the second letter out of the ribbon and passed it over. "This one will break your hearts."

Alexandra hesitated after scanning the envelope. "It's stamped May 15, 1912." She looked around the table. After seeing the Titanic articles, that date had more meaning than they would have recognized before. She took the letter out, unfolded the pages, and cleared her throat. "It's another one to her sister."

May 15, 1912

My dear Anne,

Your heartfelt letter of two weeks ago, so full of love and caring, was much appreciated. I wish I could say it helped heal my heart but, Anne, I doubt my heart will ever heal.

I am sorry I didn't stop to see you and your new baby on my way home. I know you understand.

Alexandra hesitated and looked around the table. This wasn't starting off well. She inhaled deeply to muster courage before continuing.

It has been one month to the day since being thrust into a chasm of hell like none I ever imagined. You've read the newspaper articles, many that were inaccurate at first but have since been corrected. So many innocent souls perished needlessly. And some were saved at the hands of the most selfless human beings to walk this earth, including my Roland.

Anne, I cannot sleep at night for seeing my dear husband. He guided me into a lifeboat and then rather than take a seat himself, he went back for women and children. Rich, poor, he didn't care. We saw lifeboats with the rich leaving half full at best, but my dear Roland yelled at our rower to wait until ours was full. I will never forget how commanding my husband became. There was no denying him. I only wish that had been the case for the other lifeboats. They would have left filled with survivors.

Selfishly, I screamed for him to get in. I don't know if he even heard me in the chaos and din.

One after another, he pushed women who hesitated. He took children by their hands and dropped them in. It was a mother from steerage and her three children who were the last to fill our boat. She clung to the infant in her arms as my Roland picked her up and let her down. Then he got her biggest child in. He picked up the screaming toddler left alone on the deck of the ship, stepped into the lifeboat, and settled the child into my arms.

Our hands touched. Our eyes met. Our lips kissed.

Then he stepped out of the lifeboat and hollered at our oarsman to go quickly. It was at that moment I knew I would never see my Roland again. My last glimpse of him was his back as he scurried away to help others. I knew he would never take a place in a lifeboat as long as a woman or child needed that seat. He would let himself perish before he would allow such loss.

Anne, I thought it impossible to love my husband more than I did on the day we wed. But on April 15 my heart swelled to know no bounds for true love. I will never love like that again because there is no greater love.

Do I selfishly wish he'd chosen to come home with me? Of course.

But do I know I would never have looked at him in the same adoring way if he had? I must admit, yes.

I think about those he saved. I pray they live good,

fulfilling lives. I want the loss of him to be worth something.

Because I will miss him until my dying day.

But fear not that I will entertain the thought of soon visiting him in the hereafter. For you see, my dear Roland gave me the greatest gift imaginable.

I am with child.

Ivy

No one spoke. Her hand trembling, Alexandra set down the letter and stared at it. One after another, they took tissues out of the box and dried their eyes.

"I just thought of something," Wanda croaked. "We didn't find an obituary or anything about Roland's death. It must still be up there." She pointed toward the attic.

"That or she couldn't bare keeping it," Barb suggested.

Alexandra got up and went to the other end of the table where she'd left the Rand family tree. She brought it over and sat back down. Pointing at a name, she said, "Well, we know that Ivy had a son named Gareth Rand. It was her father who gave her and Roland Rand this cottage as a wedding gift."

"Gareth was my grandfather," Barb said. "He was born and raised here on the island but left to fight in World War II and never came back to live. He was career Navy man. I didn't see him often, but I adored him. What a great fellow."

"How ironic that he was in the Navy and his father died at sea." Bernard shook his head.

"Yes, it is, isn't it," Barb agreed. "I didn't know about his dad before reading these letters, so hadn't put those two things together."

"What about the family fortune?" Alexandra boldly asked.

"Oh, gone. As far as I know, we never had any. Although,

Granddad did buy me lavish gifts and he paid for my college education. He even bought me my first car. A VW bug. I loved that car."

Alexandra said, "Ivy lived in this house until her death, then her only child, Gareth, your grandfather, sold it. All the proceeds would have gone to him. He would've made a pretty penny on the sale, but it doesn't take many generations before a family fortune is gone. I've seen it happen many times. I've had a number of clients who've been shocked to find out there was once a lot of money but it all got spent before reaching them. The Rand fortune went that way, apparently."

"So Rand is your maiden name?" Wanda asked Barb.

"Yes. I didn't change it when I married. It was a '70s thing. We have two kids but divorced fifteen years ago." She looked at Bernard, taking his measure at that news.

Bernard was fine. "How are you doing, knowing this tragedy happened in your own family?" he asked.

"I was numb at first. The first time I read that letter I bawled like a baby. Those were my great-grandparents." Barb ran a hand through her hair as if clearing her head. "I mean, to know my own great-grandmother went through this and nobody ever told me. I'm not sure my dad even knew that about his parents. He only knew his dad died young. It's mind-boggling. My heart breaks for Ivy and Roland."

"It's a reminder to us to live life to the fullest while we can ..." Wanda got cut off.

"Oh!" Madison yelped. "My baby!"

"Is it coming?" Bernard jumped out of his seat, ready to run.

"No, no. It just kicked so hard it felt like my belly would burst open."

"May I?" Wanda held out a hand.

"Ah huh."

Wanda placed her hand on Madison's swollen belly. "Oh my word! He or she is playing Whac-a-Mole in there!"

Laughter filled the room as the women took turns feeling the baby. When it came Bernard's turn, he declined. "No. No. I'm good. I'll take your word for it."

"Come on, coward," his cousin insisted. "You never had any kids.

This is your once-in-a-lifetime chance to feel a kicking baby inside a mommy's tummy."

"That's never been on my bucket list." He adamantly shook his head.

"Come on, Bernard. It's a beautiful thing," Barb coaxed.

That did it. The big old guy hefted himself out of his chair and felt the pregnant belly. "I feel it! It's kicking! It's a rowdy one!" He chortled with delight.

The cottage on the West Bluff of Mackinac Island filled with laughter and joy and the promise of new life. And in no time at all, that new life would be nestled in their arms.

CHAPTER 17

Summertime, 1847

Ian had been gone for ten years. An eternity.

He was twenty-one. He'd finished school with honors in Montreal and then completed a four-year apprenticeship with a prominent lawyer in Detroit. He had a new job, however, as a lawyer in Lansing in the center of the state, the new capital.

He would not be moving back to the island as his parents had hoped. They'd had grand plans for him to open the first law practice on Mackinac Island. But their plans were shattered upon learning he intended to stay downstate. He had his own life now and apparently it didn't include a bunch of small-town islanders he'd left behind in Lake Huron.

It was a couple of hours before he would arrive for a visit and Cassie decided to prepare by riding Doodles to her cave. The rest of the village was treating Ian's return like a big event, as if a high-and-mighty prince was coming home after years in battle. Her aunt and uncle's place, Niall's Pub, was to be the center of the celebration. Cassie refused to get all lathered up about the traitor's visit but had been coerced by her parents to promise she'd make a polite appearance, at least for a few minutes.

She rode her horse with gusto. The brisk springtime air invigorated her as Doodles trotted to their destination without needing a guiding rein. They'd visited the cave many times over the years. In fact, the mare knew every trail on the island as well as any human.

Cassie's Cave had long since revealed her life's desire. She'd mastered Chief Joe's practice of pimadaziwin, going into a dream state and beseeching her ancestors to speak to her. And they did, supporting her wish to be a wife and mother. She wanted to be a good neighbor. She wanted to participate in her community. But she wanted to do all that as a partner to a man, not as his possession as she witnessed in some marriages. She wanted a marriage like those in her family where men and women treated each other equally.

Would she ever find that on her island? Or would she have to sacrifice and give up this sacred place for the sake of a good marriage? Or might she never find that kind of love at all? She had no answers and her ancestors left those questions for her to figure out on her own. They told her that the answers she sought were within her, echoing what Chief Joe had said so long ago.

The chief had died a year after leaving the island. They discovered he'd been ninety-nine years old.

She sat on a rock beside her small cave, thinking of what a gift the chief had been to her and to so many others. Her mind wandered and she thought about her plight. She might never marry. Her wish to be a mother might never come true. She might become an old maid. Eventually, her fretting spent, she turned her attention to her surroundings. "Live now," her ancestors insisted. She scanned the area and marveled at how small her cave was. It wasn't a cave as much as an impression in a boulder. When she was a child, it seemed enormous.

"Well, Ian will be home any minute." She stood and approached her friend, stroking her neck. She adored talking to Doodles, who seldom disagreed. "What do you think will happen? Will he bring a fiancé? Maybe even a wife, huh? Maybe he has a child by now, one he's been keeping secret from us."

Doodles whinnied, turned her broad backside to Cassie, and wandered off to eat fresh spring grass and wildflowers.

"Oh. You don't think so? Hmmm. I probably won't even like him anymore. Remember when he came home when I was eleven? I had the measles and had to stay in the loft. When I was fourteen, he came for a month that summer and treated me like I had the plague. I'm not expecting him to be nice to me this time around either."

The animal raised its head and snorted.

Doodles always put Cassie in a better mood when she was feeling down. "Come, my love," she said. "How about we take a fast run through the island?"

Doodles nodded vigorously and Cassie hopped on. A lively ride always made her feel happy, no matter what strange things were happening in her world.

Like her cousin Ian coming home to visit.

She reached the pub late, the celebration having already begun. Boisterous laughter could be heard by the time she reached the edge of town. Leaving Doodles in her stable at the house, she walked the short distance to the pub. When she opened the door, all heads turned to stare. Silence struck like that when a hymn ends in church. The crowd parted to make way between her and the village's native son, the high-falutin' lawyer.

There he was, standing in the center of the room, glass of ale in hand, holding court. She stepped inside, leaving the door open behind her. Rays of sunshine billowed into the room, giving her an ethereal glow.

He looked like a different person. She hardly recognized the lad she'd known. This was no boy. It was a man. A very beguiling man, she had to admit.

Even when he'd last visited at age seventeen, he hadn't looked like this. He'd grown six inches. She had to stretch her neck to see his face. He wore a white shirt, black vest, and black pants. His black boots were shiny. Shiny! Pfft. Those boots had never seen an honest day's work.

And here she stood in a plain dress, her Odawa belt, and riding boots. Her black hair with its fiery highlights had gone the way of the wind as she rode. She tucked a wayward strand behind her ear.

His unruly black hair, inherited from his pa, was neatly combed. His face was clean-shaven. His blue eyes as bright as a morning sky, however, hadn't changed. They were the only recognizable part of him. She would have known them anywhere.

"Ah! There she is," he declared. He gestured with the glass in his hand and approached. "Cassie. Hello."

That was it? That was all he had to say to her? She looked around. At least she didn't see a wife hanging onto his arm or bairns clinging to his pantlegs.

"Hello, Ian."

"It's good to see you."

"Huh." All eyes were on them. She struggled to come up with something civil to say. "How was your journey home?"

"It was fine. It's an easy trip these days with new roads."

"I see. That must explain why you've come home to visit so very often." She couldn't help herself. When he'd been so far away in Montreal, Canada, it had been understandable that he wouldn't often make it back home. But for the last four years he'd been right in the heart of the lower peninsula of Michigan in Lansing. Surely, he could've made it home at least once a year.

"Cassie Colleen," her pa interjected, his tone conciliatory. "Your cousin has made a long journey to visit his family and friends. We must welcome him home."

"Of course, Pa." She glared at Ian. "Welcome home after your excruciatingly long and arduous journey home to see your family who has done naught but love and support you."

Pa huffed in exasperation. Ma struggled to keep a straight face. Everyone else held their breath.

It was Aunt Saoirse who came to Cassie, put an arm around her waist, and ushered her away from the door. "Come, my dear. We've got a wee celebration with rum cake and whisky."

"I'll have whisky," Cassie commanded.

Pa rolled his eyes. Ma snickered out loud.

And Ian ... Well, Ian strode up to his cousin, held his glass of ale out of the way, wrapped his other arm around her waist, drew her into him, and kissed her on the lips.

She stiffened and placed her palms on his chest to push him off her. Her mouth, however, had somehow, of its own volition, molded to the kiss.

He backed away and cheered, "Welcome home to me!" He raised his glass in a toast and took a long swig.

"Hear, hear!" others shouted as they, too, imbibed.

Cassie McIntyre hauled off to smack him for his brashness but, unlike the time she walloped him when they were kids, he caught her wrist. "Ah, ah, ah. Not this time," he said. "Now why would you want to be fighting with the man who's come all this way on this – let me see, what was it? Oh, this 'excruciatingly long and arduous journey' to see you?"

"To see me?" She backed away and scanned the room. Dozens of pairs of curious eyes bore into her. She stumbled into a chair and corrected herself, pulling in her waist and lifting her chest to prove she had control of herself.

"Yes, you," he asserted. He held out his free hand. "To ask for your hand – not the one that only moments ago wanted to pummel me, ..." the crowd erupted in laughter "... the other one. To ask for that hand in marriage." He pointed at her left hand.

She panicked. This wasn't how it was supposed to go. She'd dreamt about a marriage proposal ever since reading novels like *Pride and Prejudice* where Darcy and Elizabeth became engaged in a tender and romantic scene. Her fantasy for her own proposal was a beautiful moonlit night by the shore. She and the man of her dreams would be alone for an amorous tete-a-tete. They would kiss rapturously, he'd get down on one knee, and he'd present her with a gold Claddagh ring, an Irish tradition. Her former suiters hadn't hit the mark but at least they'd been better than this.

"You're proposing to me in a pub?" She was aghast with disbelief. "With the whole village watching?"

"I figured it'd be harder for you to say no this way."

"Well, it isn't. Harder, I mean. To say no. I can say no all I want."

A chorus of groans arose from the crowd. They were disappointed. Apparently, unbeknownst to her, the entire village had long expected to see them wed.

"Aw, come on now, lassie," some fellow beseeched. "Give the poor sap a chance."

"Is that your answer?" Ian quipped. "No?"

She lifted her chin in defiance. "No. I mean, I don't know yet what my answer will be."

"Ah, she needs to think about it." Ian turned a circle to address the whole room. "I'm thinking that's not a good sign. I believe I will need your help." He took a long swig of his ale.

Folks began to entreaty her to say yes but she cut them short. "Stop! I will decide for myself. Now, let me consider this … person … before us." She put her hands on her hips and sashayed around Ian. "He's good looking enough, I suppose."

"He's gorgeous!" an old woman hollered.

The crowd erupted in laughter and lifted their glasses in agreement.

"And," Cassie said, eyeing him up and down, "I suppose he's smart enough."

"A lawyer, no less!" a man declared. "He'll talk their heads off in court and end up rich, lassie."

The villagers guffawed.

"Those boots, however." She scoffed. "Has he ever done an honest day's work?"

The crowd gave her that one and their cheering disintegrated into "ahs" and "ohs."

"I'll need some promises from you – if I decide I want to wed you." Cassie stabbed a finger at Ian's chest. "Now. In front of all these witnesses." In a dramatic flair, she swept out an arm to take in the room.

"Anything, my love," he said, clearly entertained by the whole ordeal. He placed one hand in the small of his back and stood at attention. Half-attention, actually, as he seemed reticent to let go of his stout brew.

As for Cassie, she spread her feet in a stable stance and counted on her fingers. "First of all, if I grant you the honor of marrying me, we will return to the island each summer to visit our families and friends."

"That is a splendid idea. I've missed my hometown and the people in it." He held his glass high then took a swig.

"Secondly, we will not live in the city but in the countryside near the city."

"Agreed." Another gulp.

"Thirdly, you will not try to prohibit me from riding my horse whenever I please."

"I would not dream of trying to prohibit you from doing anything you want to do. I know better." This time he took a long draw and the adoring crowd noisily joined in.

She squinted suspiciously. "One more thing. Number four." The room went still. She held up four fingers. "I will wear my Odawa belt with pride." She ran her hands along her belt. "I am proud of my heritage. Odawa, French, and English by blood. Irish by love. If your fancy friends in the city don't like that, they can be damned."

Ian studied her without saying anything. The silence in the pub became eerily foreboding as villagers waited for a response.

A flash of fear struck Cassie when it seemed he might change his mind and walk out. But his mouth slowly curled upward until forming a full grin that caused his eyes to glint with merriment. He handed off his glass, went to her, fingered her belt, and said, "Let them be damned."

Her old Ian was back! Cassie threw her arms around his neck. "Yes, I will marry you!"

They kissed again as the crowd erupted in hoots and hollers. The couple was quickly surrounded and congratulated. It was an hour before they managed to get away.

They walked to a secluded spot on the shore. The big lake, calm as glass, mirrored fluffy white clouds in the sky. They paused to take in the spectacular view.

"Cassie," Ian said, "I have a confession. I tried to stop loving you. I tried to love another. But I couldn't. When I was ten years old, I told you I wanted to marry you. No one has ever able to make me change my mind, no matter how hard they tried."

She faced him and took his hand in hers. "I could never say yes to other suiters, either. I thought I should. I thought I shouldn't even think of you, seeing that we're cousins. But we aren't really, are we."

"No. We are not related by blood. I'm afraid I rudely revealed that to you when we were children when I told you your pa was in the post cemetery. I'm so sorry I hurt you but I'm so glad it's true."

Before she could respond, Ian dropped down on one knee, took a small velvet box out of his pocket, and opened it to reveal a gold Claddagh ring set with a small garnet gem. "Cassie McIntyre, I am officially asking you to make my life complete by agreeing to be my wife." He took the ring out of the box and held it out to her.

She lifted her hand and he slipped the ring on her finger. "Yes, Ian. I will be honored to be your wife," she whispered as her eyes misted.

It turned out, she now knew, the most fantastic dreams could come true.

CHAPTER 18

*A*utumn, 2023

September 1, 1912

Dearest Anne,

    The most miraculous thing has happened. In my deep sorrow and despair over the loss of my Roland, I've met an old woman who has bolstered my courage and whittled away at my fear of raising a child without a father. Her name is Cassandra Colleen McIntyre. Everyone on the island calls her Miss Cassie.

Wanda's voice rose to a fevered pitch as she read the third and final letter. "It's our Cassandra!" She pointed at Madison to indicate hers, too. "What?" She held the letter out in disbelief. "Barb, your ancestor, who lived in this very house, and ours knew each other!"

"I didn't know that. I've read this letter many times and had no idea." Barb shook her head in wonder.

"This is fantastic," Alexandra said. "It makes sense, though, because

99

even in the early 1900s the island still had a small permanent population. Maybe seven hundred people. It makes sense that if both women lived here, they would've run into each other."

"Let's see … how old would Cassandra have been?" Wanda wanted to know.

"She was born in 1830," Alexandra noted. She pointed at the date stamped on the envelope, September 1, 1912 … "so in 1912 she was eighty-two. She lived a good long life."

"They called her Cassie instead of Cassandra, so I think we should, too." Madison leaned over her belly and slid her forearms onto the table to get closer to the amazing letter. "Read more, please."

Miss Cassie is the widow of a fine gentlemen who was a lawyer and state senator for many years. They lived on a farm outside of Lansing and had five children, now scattered around the country with their own children. She moved back to her hometown here on the island when her husband died and she became too old to handle the farm alone. Although she has a large family of her own, she has kindly "adopted" me, she says, because she loves me. It's that simple.

"We knew my four-times-great-grandmother lived in Lansing," Wanda said. "But we didn't know any of this about her husband."

"I'll do some research on him," Alexandra offered. "Interesting fellow."

Anne, to meet someone who is so generous and kind, who loves others with such abandon, is one of the greatest gifts I've ever received. She reassures me I will rise to the task of raising my child alone, although she titters when admitting there will be trying days. She tells me I am stronger than I know because women are stronger than they have been raised to believe. That strength is already within me, she says, and will rise to the surface when needed. She and so many others in the village will be here to help and support me. I need not do this alone.

Wanda paused and glanced at Madison. The girl was deep in thought, emboldened by her ancestor's words. She sat up straighter. Her shoulders squared. Her face transformed from that of a forsaken teenager to a confident young woman. They smiled at one another and Wanda went back to reading.

I now know that my decision to stay here on the island permanently was the best decision I could make. We're isolated, remote, and interdependent. I only hope that someday I can return the favor of the kindness I receive here. It will be my mission to do so.

Bernard chimed in with, "It's still like that here. There's that feeling of community, of knowing someone will always be there to help you out."

"Like you fixing the hinge on our gate." Wanda reached over to pat his hand.

"Aw, that's nothing. It keeps me busy."

Wanda returned to the letter.

I must confess, dear Anne, that having high society folks here on the island for the summer was trying for me. With so many cottages now lining the bluffs and in town, the rich descend upon the island for a month or two during good weather. I know, I know We're rich, too. But having been away from the "upper crust" and having

*spent more time with islanders, I find that the expecta-
tions of manners and protocols and requirements to fit in
are exhausting. Even the clothes are exhausting. I often
used being in a family way as an excuse to decline
dinner and party invitations. It seemed that those I did
attend were overwhelmed by people who wanted to brag
about having known my Roland and what a hero he had
been.*

I know he was a hero. He was always my hero.

*Miss Cassie taught me the most wonderful thing. I
am afraid the name escapes me, as it's a long Odawa
word. Did I tell you she has Odawa heritage? It starts
with "pinada..." something. It's a belief that if you open
yourself up to "dream visitors," your ancestors, they will
bless you with a fulfilling and happy life if you are
worthy. These ancestors already live within you, so you
always have access to that blessing if you open your
heart and soul to the wisdom that has been passed down
to you.*

Madison had pulled her phone out of her pocket and searched.
"Here it is. 'Pima-dazi-win. An Odawa traditional belief that if one
walks in the path of their ancestors with an honest and worthy life,
they can ask ancestor dream visitors to bless their life to be long and
free of misfortune.'"

"That's beautiful. Thanks, Madison. Our ancestor was clearly
impressed with that idea." Wanda read on.

*The Odawa believe that ancestors from the past seven
generations lived their lives with us, their descendants, in*

mind. Therefore, we must live with the next seven generations in mind in all we do. We must be stewards of the earth, animals, and each other. Isn't that lovely?

I took a long walk the other day and came upon the small cave in the middle of the island where Miss Cassie told me she likes to go to visit with her ancestors. She calls it Cassie's Cave, naturally. It drew me to it like a magnet, seeming the perfect place to sit quietly and invite my dream visitors to join me. Once I quieted my mind, there they were, Anne, inside me. My heart swelled with joy at knowing my child and I will always have their love and guidance. And we will live fulfilling lives. I will make certain of it for my child.

When I told Miss Cassie this, she gave me a beautiful, beaded Odawa belt made for her by her mother and grandmother. I objected to taking such a treasure, suggesting she give it to someone in her family. She said she and her mother had made such belts for each of her daughters and granddaughters. I took it with delight and wear it as I write. It brings me peace.

I know you may think I've lost my mind. I'm sure our Methodist minister would think so. But I've come to accept many ways of embracing life since Roland lost his life. Being here on the island has guided me along the way.

Your upcoming visit with your daughter is anxiously awaited. Five months old already! I cannot wait to hug my niece. You, too, my dear sister. With the Detroit & Mackinac Railway running directly from your city to our *island ferry, we must take advantage of it and visit both ways more often.*

Loving regards,

Ivy

"I know right where that cave is," Bernard declared. "There are others but the one more in the center of the island is Skull Cave."

"Yes, it's called Skull Cave because it's believed that long ago there was a native burial ground inside." Alexandra pointed toward its location.

"I wonder if our Cassie knew that," Madison pondered.

"Can we go there?" Barb asked.

"Sure." Bernard took his phone out of the pocket of his overalls. "I'll call my friend Eddie. He has a private carriage. He shouldn't be too busy this time of year. Everybody want to go?"

He got affirmations all around.

The horse-drawn carriage arrived at the cottage half an hour later. They all hopped in, except for Madison, of course, who rather rolled her way in. Eddie, a brawny young man of about twenty-five, helped her up and made sure she was settled. They took off for Skull Cave, Cassie's Cave to them. On the way, Bernard explained to Eddie what their mission was all about. When they arrived, everyone remained silently seated in the carriage at first, taking in the essence of the large limestone rock with the broad opening to a shallow cave that had been so important to their ancestors. When they got down and stood in front of it, Eddie read the historical marker aloud.

"According to tradition this is the cave in which the English fur-trader Alexander Henry hid out during the Indian uprising of 1763. The floor of the cave, he claimed, was covered with human bones, presumably Indian."

"Spooky," Barb said. "I love it."

Genealogist Alexandra had a different take on it. "Maybe they were the bones of the very ancestors Miss Cassie and Ivy sought."

A wood fence with a sign that warned "No Climbing" barred them from entering the cave. Instead, they leaned on the fence and took in the scenery for a while.

Eventually, they headed home. Wanda offered to fix supper for everyone, Eddie included. Bernard insisted on grilling some ribs he had on hand. Barb claimed she made a mean salad. Alexandra pointed out the fresh loaf of sourdough bread she'd made and brought over earlier.

The men went next door to Bernard's to get the ribs on the grill, Wanda busied herself making iced tea and getting out everything Barb needed for the salad, and Alexandra sat on a stool clicking at her phone to research Cassie Colleen's husband, Ian McIntyre, lawyer and senator. Madison went to the front porch to lie down on the swing and take a nap.

Dinner would be served in due time. But according to island time, there was no rush.

CHAPTER 19

*S*ummertime, 1847

Doodles ran like the wind as Cassie hung on with glee. This would be her last ride on the island before her marriage to Ian the next day, and she was on a mission before moving away.

They would be leaving the island immediately after their vows, as Ian had to get back to his law practice. He had a court case coming up in a week.

She pulled in on the reins when they reached the post cemetery where soldiers from the fort were buried. Doodles fussed, knowing it wasn't a regular stop. Cassie hadn't visited this burial ground since she'd been seven years old, the time she'd come looking for her father's grave. Today something urged her say goodbye to the mystery man. She had something she needed to say to him.

Even though there were more crosses now, the location of his cross was seared into her brain. She dismounted and went straight to it. She glared down at the grave of the man who'd made half of her.

"Hello, Private Harold Smith. You no doubt do not remember me. I am your child but in blood only. I don't know you and you don't know me. Still, I've come to say goodbye. I'm moving away but will be visiting the island in the future. However, I don't intend to come here to visit you again. You see, I don't much like you. In fact, I don't like you at all. I will never forget the pain in my mother's eyes ten years ago when I asked her to tell me about you. You were not good to her. Although she's never spoken a word of it, I know it without fail. And for that, I despise you. I know God says to forgive. Perhaps someday I will. But not today. I hope you are where you belong, rotting in Hell at the hands of Satan.

"Oh, by the by, my dear mother, Gichigama Geneviève St. Croix, the woman you mistreated, has been married for many long years to a wonderful man. He's an Irishman. How do you like that? I know you hate the Irish. Well, think of this. He has enjoyed her warmth and love all these many years that you've been lying here in the hard, cold ground.

"Mr. Liam McIntyre. He is my real father, my pa. Not you.

"Good-bye, Mr. Smith."

She fled and jumped onto Doodles who, sensing her need, took off in a gallop. She'd been wanting to talk to Harold Smith ever since becoming a woman. When a child, after her one visit to the cemetery, she'd merely wanted to pretend he'd never existed. Maturity had shown her that acknowledging him had no impact on her life. He made no difference.

Still, it felt good to speak her mind to him. She'd been saying goodbye to friends and family in preparation for her departure after becoming a married woman. Harold Smith had been her final farewell.

She had one more thing left to do and thrilled at the jaunty ride to her cave. Once inside, she sat on the ground with her back up against the limestone wall and closed her eyes. Breathing rhythmically, she allowed the silence to fill her body with peace. It didn't take long to sense her ancestors around her, infusing her body, embracing and guiding her.

"You're happy I'm marrying Ian, aren't you?"

The answer didn't come in words but in a warm sensation in her chest.

"I know you'll be with me no matter where I go, but I'll miss our cave."

They would miss it, too, but would always be with her. Her new adventure excited them.

"I hope it's a good adventure. It sure will be different. But I know I can do it, especially with Ian at my side. I hope we have lots of happy children." She grinned at the thought.

Her ancestors were pleased.

"Sometimes I wonder about our children, and their children, and their children, seven generations down, like Chief Joe said. I wonder if they'll know anything about me. I hope they at least understand that I was here on this earth and that I love them with all my heart even though we will never meet in the flesh. I hope they love me the way I love you."

If her ancestors could present themselves in physical form, she knew that at that moment they would be crying with joy. She could feel their ethereal hugs.

"Good-bye for now. Next time, we'll meet in Lansing. I know you will be with me there."

Doodles took a slow route home, walking along as if the world held not one care. It made Cassie feel carefree and grateful for her life.

By the time they reached town, she felt renewed and ready to embark on her new life.

CHAPTER 20

*A*utumn, 2023

They ate at the picnic table on the front lawn. Wanda always preferred the front yard because of the spectacular view of Lake Huron, the Mackinac Bridge, and Lake Michigan beyond. They watched the sun set over the water, offering a radiant array of colors splayed across the sky and reflected on the lake. The solar lights James had strung from tree to tree came on, giving the evening a warm glow.

They reviewed all they had learned from Ivy's letters and marveled at the revelations. They talked about knowing that Ivy's son had a good life, as he'd been Barb's grandfather who she remembered well, a jolly fellow she'd adored. Alexandra had earlier prepared Barb's family tree, which revealed that Ivy had died an old woman, by all accounts content with her island existence.

They also discussed their passion for Mackinac Island life. Alexandra and Eddie had lived there all their lives. Neither could imagine ever living anywhere else, although they liked to travel for vacations. Eddie had gone to Michigan State University and had a degree in animal science. His aim was to build a business of island tours with half a dozen horses and carriages and drivers who were tour guides.

When Bernard asked Madison if she had a career goal in mind yet, she hesitated. "Well, I'm kinda embarrassed 'cuz I don't know how this could ever happen, seeing that I'll have, you know …" she pointed at her belly "… a baby to take care of. But I've thought about it a lot and I wanna be an EMT. An emergency medical technician."

Wanda shot a look at Alexandra, who threw back a slight nod. They'd both noticed that Madison had just said she'd be taking care of her own baby, meaning the option for adoption had apparently fallen by the wayside. Wanda wondered if Madison was even consciously aware of how her thinking was changing, an interesting development.

"Tell them the rest about what you want to do," Wanda coaxed good-naturedly.

Madison let loose with a wide smile. "I wanna drive the ambulance. I've always wanted to drive a big truck."

"Bravo!" Bernard cheered with a slap to the table. "That's a great career goal."

Eddie said, "The only motor vehicles allowed on the island are the ambulance and a police car that only get used when there's an emergency. You could work right here."

"Don't say you don't know how you're going to do it," Wanda soothed. "Remember, our Cassie Colleen and her friend Ivy taught us that anything is possible. We'll help you find a way."

"Hear, hear," Alexandra agreed. "We'll take it one thing at a time and get it done. Starting with a baby."

As the night wore on, Bernard and Barb wandered over to his porch to have a nightcap. It turned out they both had an affinity for Maker's Mark bourbon.

Alexandra left for home on her bike, a flashlight in the basket to serve as a headlight in the dark. Her trek was a short mile or so to the small village of Hendersonville, inland on the island.

When Eddie said goodbye and headed for his carriage, Madison stopped him. "Eddie, Aunt Wanda, let's visit the cave again."

"In the dark?" Wanda understood being drawn to the cave but not without daylight.

"Yes."

"I'll take you." Eddie didn't hesitate. "I love roaming around the island in the dark. With so little ambient light, the night sky is awesome. It's a lot like it would've been when your ancestors were here."

The all looked up at the starlit sky, the Milky way clearly visible in its dazzling display. Wanda had always thought it looked like God had taken a handful of stars and planets and tossed them out into the universe to adorn the night sky with glory.

"Okay. We may as well." Wanda agreed knowing that if James was there, he'd jump at the chance for this little adventure.

Once they reached the cave, Madison tumbled out of the carriage and headed straight for the fence.

"Honey," Wanda called, "it says, 'No Climbing.'"

"I know." Madison lifted a leg and tried to climb over. She fell back and tried again. Eddie rushed to her and without a word cupped her butt to help her haul herself over. "Thanks," she said. "I won't be long. You two stay there. Please." She pointed back at the carriage. "I want to be alone in there."

The young man joined Wanda by the carriage. They gawked as Madison pulled out her phone and turned on the flashlight and disappeared into the black mouth of the cave.

"I watched you tonight," Wanda said. "If I'm not mistaking, you're a bit smitten with my niece."

"I am."

She liked his straightforwardness. "I don't think she's in the mood right now to be courted. She's a bit busy and will be for quite a while."

"I'm a patient man."

"A lot of men wouldn't have anything to do with a pregnant girl."

"A lot of men are idiots."

She snickered. "Ain't that the truth. She's only sixteen, you know. She'll be seventeen in a couple of weeks."

"I can wait."

"So you've said. Okay then. Take it easy and if she likes you, I will, too."

He graced her with such a magnificent smile she couldn't resist. She already liked him.

They didn't talk anymore as they stared at the sky. After fifteen minutes, Madison came out and Eddie helped her back over the fence.

"You okay, honey?" Wanda asked.

Madison took a last look at the cave. "Yes. I'm good. I had to go talk to our ancestors."

She didn't offer any more information, so no one pried. They rode home is silence, enjoying the sound of the clip-clop of the horse, an owl's hoot every now and then, and the awareness of how things used to be.

CHAPTER 21

*S*ummertime, 1847

Early the next day, the marriage ceremony took place at Ste. Anne's Catholic Church, the church the bride and the groom had attended every Sunday of their youth and that Cassie still attended. It was where her parents had wed, as well. They invited the whole village, so the log building was full to bursting.

"You are so beautiful!" Ian exclaimed for all to hear when Cassie came to his side at the altar. The congregation chuckled, as that wasn't part of the ceremony. The priest cleared his throat in disapproval. Everyone settled down at the gesture of disfavor from the man of God.

Cassie wore her mother's fringed, white Odawa wedding dress with its lace nod to Americanization. Her beaded belt enwrapped her slender waist. Ma had styled her long hair atop her head, secured with a gemstone comb willed to her by Madame La Framboise, who'd died a year earlier. The matriarch's largesse was much appreciated and she was greatly missed by many.

Usually able to divert her mind to an entertaining story when mass became long and dull, this time Cassie only wanted one story, her love story with Ian. The nuptial mass seemed interminable. All she wanted to do was make Ian her husband. Finally, the priest had them repeat their vows and it was done. The guests made sure to remain respectfully quiet in the house of God as the bride and groom departed.

Raucous gaiety came afterward at a gathering at the pub, which included so many people it spilled out into the street. Most revelers didn't notice when only half an hour later the bride and groom left to go to the dock.

Theirs parents, siblings, and grandmothers trailed along, the elder women being aided by canes and the arms of strong, young grandsons.

Their few trunks were already loaded onto the good-sized boat hired by Ian. Doodles, skittish and displeased, and a dray were onboard, too. They would go to the mainland and begin their journey to Lansing. It would take a week to get there. Ian knew of inns they could stay at along the way.

It was by far the furthest away from home Cassie had ever been. She'd traveled by canoe to St. Ignace on the northern shore and to where Fort Michilimackinac had once stood on the southern shore. Her entire life had revolved around the Straits of Mackinac. Lansing, the capital in the center of the state, was a big city she'd only imagined from storybooks. Ian said its population was 1,100 people. She couldn't imagine such a thing.

It would be a new way of life with her husband and Cassie McIntyre was up for the challenge. Especially with Ian, her best friend, at her side.

CHAPTER 22

*D*ecember 24, 2023

The wedding took place in front of the fireplace in Wanda and James's cottage, the crackling flames a charming backdrop. It was where they'd married one year earlier. As before, this was a lovely, heartwarming ceremony.

The women had spent days decorating the house in a joyful array of pine boughs, cream-colored satin ribbons, gold and silver bulbs, twinkling lights, and a live blue spruce Christmas tree. A garland wrapped the stair rail and another spanned the mantle. Mistletoe hung in the doorway to the living room. Lighted white candles in crystal glass holders flickered around the room, and two lanterns nestled in the garland on the mantle. The scent of fresh pine filled the air.

The large picture window framed an expansive view of a fairytale land covered in billowy white, leafless trees laden with snow, and the swirling designs of evolving ice skimming the enormous blue lake. Scattered clouds languidly dropped crystal snowflakes that sparkled in sporadic beams of sunlight.

It was a magical day.

With so few in attendance – Wanda, James, Alexandra, Madison, Barb, Bernard, and Eddie – everyone except the couple getting married served as a bridesmaid or best man. They stood around the happy couple.

Barb and Bernard, the bride and groom, beamed as they clasped hands. She looked radiant in a stunning lavender dress. He looked like a fine gentleman in a black suit and lavender tie. Wanda had never seen him in anything but overalls. She was impressed.

James looked dapper himself. Wanda was thrilled to have him by her side. While he'd been gone on his three-week trip to Antarctica, she'd missed him more than she could have imagined. Thankfully, she'd had the stories of Cassie McIntyre and Ivy Rand and Madison's situation to keep her occupied.

Her heart swelled with love for her husband, so much so it spilled out into the whole world. The past year had been the happiest of her adult life, and she knew it would only get better as she and James created fond memories and a loving future.

James took his wife's hand when the officiant, an elderly retired preacher, asked the bride, "Barb, do you take this man to be your wedded husband to cherish always, honor and sustain in sickness and in health, in poverty and in wealth, until death alone shall part you?"

Barb opened her mouth to reply but ...

"Ah-h-h!" Madison screamed.

Everyone turned to look at the teen, whose head was bent as she pulled up her long skirt enough to see the puddle on the floor between her feet. She looked up in sheer terror.

"It's coming," she whispered, her voice raw.

"The baby!" Alexandra hollered.

"But, but ..." the officiant stammered.

"I do!" Barb yelped.

"Me, too!" Bernard declared.

"I now pronounce you husband and wife. You may kiss .... Oh, never mind." The old preacher gave up.

The women scrambled around Madison and helped her lie down

on the sofa. They had rehearsed this moment and James had the task of calling the doctor. Their next move was to have been a trip to the clinic, but Wanda took one look at Madison and announced they'd never make it. She hollered at James to tell the doctor to come to the house. He ran into the kitchen to make the call away from all the commotion.

Wanda ordered Eddie to run upstairs and bring back a clean sheet and blanket. He dashed up the stairs, the linen closet door could be heard slamming open, and he came back with four sheets and three blankets. The women helped Madison get a sheet underneath her and covered her legs with the blanket. The teen cried out numerous times while they got her settled.

Bernard went to the kitchen for a rag and cleaned up the floor.

Wanda clutched her niece's hand. Madison's death grip hurt, but she wasn't about to say anything.

The men left the room to give the girl some privacy. As nervous as if they were having the baby, they huddled around the kitchen table, nibbled on the reception snacks, and drank coffee.

It only took ten minutes before a snowmobile could be heard outside. Eddie jumped up and went to the door to let the doctor in. The M.D. went straight into the living room to the mother-to-be. Eddie hesitated but retreated back to the kitchen.

Half an hour later a wail worthy of a warrior goddess filled the cottage. Madison delivered a baby girl who sported a head full of frowzled red hair. The three older women cried with joy. Madison held her newborn to her chest and stared at its tiny pink face in amazement.

"She's the most beautiful baby in the world!" the new mother declared.

Wanda laughed. "Yes, she is."

"She certainly is, sweet pea," Alexandra cooed.

Barb smiled. "Why, there's never been a prettier baby."

The men rejoined them and everyone marveled at the tiny Christmas miracle in their midst.

Wanda stroked the baby's hair. "Madison, what are you going to name her."

The teen kissed her newborn's forehead, looked up at the grownups, and said, "Her name is Ivy Colleen."

CHAPTER 23

*S*ummertime, 1927

Ninety-seven-year-old Cassie McIntyre, known to everyone on the island as Miss Cassie, sat on the shore of Lake Michigan contemplating her life. It had been a good, long life. She'd borne five children who'd scattered around the country and made good lives for themselves and their families. She had eight grandchildren and a dozen great-grandchildren. Three generations down.

She wondered about the four generations yet to come. Having lived her entire adult life with seven generations of her descendants in mind, as Chief Joe taught her to do, she would watch over them when she went to Heaven. Of that she felt certain.

As much as she loved and adored her offspring, she had long ago admitted to herself and to God that the best part of her life had been her earthly love affair with her Ian. Their passion for each other had been a fantastic surprise on their wedding night. Neither had known such pleasures existed. As the years went by, those pleasures grew not only in body but in mind, heart, and soul, as well.

Now that he was gone and her children had their own lives, she was ready to leave this earth she so loved. She was ready to be with her Ian again.

There was only one thing that kept her tied to life on earth. In 1912, she'd met a young woman named Ivy Rand, a widow whose child she'd helped deliver. It was a momentous event, what with Ivy's husband having drowned eight and a half months earlier on the Titanic. For the past fifteen years, Cassie had counted Ivy and her son Gareth as her own family. Watching Gareth grow up had been a delight. Now he would be off to college in a couple of years. Ivy would be fine in her beloved cottage on the West Bluff.

Cassie breathed a sigh of relief. She'd heard people talk about the work they'd done in their lives. She didn't think of it as work. All of it – the pleasures and in the end even the sorrows for the lessons they'd provided – had been a joy, a gift for which she would feel eternally grateful.

How lucky she had been to come from Mackinac Island. She'd seen many changes over the years. She was of Native, French, and English descent and raised in an Irish environment, a rich heritage no longer common. Her family had lived in a clapboard house on Main Street, now Victorian-era three-story buildings with stores, restaurants, pubs, and inns. There had been automobiles on the island for a brief time in the late 1800s, but they'd quickly been banned because they scared the horses. Now the throwback to a quieter, slower-paced time without noisy automobiles was a big draw to tourists seeking respite from a frenzied world. They came on large pleasure boats and filled the inns and boarding houses during the summertime. The Grand Hotel, an enormous, luxury hotel with the longest porch in the country, brought in visitors in droves.

Ian, a senator of renowned leadership ability, had kept his word and taken time off each summer when the Michigan State Legislature was not in session so they could visit their families and friends on the island. Her brilliant, esteemed husband's work in helping develop and refine their new state had swelled Cassie's pride in him more than she could have ever predicted when she'd married him because he was her best friend.

Their farm outside of Lansing had become her home but Mack-inac Island would always be her treasured hometown. After the children flew the coop and Ian died, she'd known she needed to sell the farm and move back to the island. She'd mourned the loss of her white farmhouse, the land, the red barn, and especially her animals. She'd helped birth many a foal, kid goat, puppy, and kitten over the years. The chickens took care of themselves.

She'd even become an unofficial midwife, somehow managing to be the only woman around when women went into labor. She hadn't set out to deliver children but was glad to have been of help. Those days were over, too, however, as a woman nowadays went to a hospital for the birth of her child.

It took a while but once the move back to the island was made, she had no regrets. Despite all the changes there over the years – it was no longer the land of her youth, but her youth was no longer, as well – it felt like coming home to where she belonged at this time of her life.

Forging new friendships and rediscovering old ones had helped. But now the time to leave forever was near. She was an ancient woman whose body was tired. It wanted to rest. It had earned that rest.

She looked out over the great lake and inhaled its life-giving fresh air. Soon it would be time for her to take her last breath. She would be laid to rest next to her Ian in Ste. Anne's Cemetery.

First, though, she decided on a whim, she would take one last walk to Cassie's Cave, her cave. It would take a while, as her gait had slowed considerably in the past few years. A memory of riding Doodles and the two of them sailing across the island trails flashed through her mind. She chuckled. She looked forward to seeing Doodles and so many others, beast and human, in the Great Beyond.

She started on her trek, happy and full of gratefulness for the life she'd shared with so many. Step by belabored step, she journeyed to her final destination.

CHAPTER 24

June, 2024

"It's time, little one, to start meeting your ancestors. Don't you think?"

Five-month-old Ivy, straddled to Madison in a baby carrier backpack, cooed at her mom. Madison put on the brakes, got off her bicycle, and leaned it against the end of the fence in front of Cassie's Cave. Ever so carefully, she took off the backpack, set it down on a patch of grass, and lifted out little Ivy. As she did so, Ivy let loose with a long string of drool that dribbled onto her blouse, leaving a slobbery streak. Madison cradled her baby in one arm, used the other hand to grab a small towel out of the basket of her bike, wiped Ivy's mouth, and dabbed at the spot on her blouse. No use. The dark menace was there to stay until it hit the washing machine.

Giving up, she threw the towel over her shoulder. Stains on her clothes had become par for the course, part of being a mother who loved the our-of-doors and took her teething infant everywhere with her.

"This is the cave of your ancestor, love," she said, rustling Ivy's wispy russet hair.

She went to the secret spot behind a bush that Eddie had cleared and slid past the end of the fence. The cave was off limits to the public. But considering it had been so important to her many-times great-grandmother, she felt like she should be allowed to visit. She always came at sunrise so island visitors wouldn't be around and think they should take liberties, too.

"Her name was Miss Cassie," she explained to her child as she entered the cave. "Cassandra Colleen Smith McIntyre. She died in this very cave in 1927. I found an old newspaper article about it. Her friend who you're named after, Ivy Rand, found her here and half the village came to escort her body into town, she was so well loved. She was an amazing woman who must never be forgotten."

Ivy grabbed her mother's lower lip and chortled with delight. Madison gently removed the little hand that had a death grip on her mouth.

"When you get older," she continued, "I'll tell you what I know about her. There is much that will help you in your life. It certainly has helped me."

She sat down on the ground with her back to the rock wall and sat Ivy on her lap facing the interior of the cave. The child instantly reached down, grabbed a pebble, and beelined it toward her mouth. Madison grabbed it, wiped it off on her jeans, and gave it back. It was too big to get into her tiny mouth so the mom needn't worry about that, and Ivy was delighted to drool all over it.

"Okay, honey, it's time to start."

Ivy cranked her chubby little neck to look back up at her mom, aware of the change in the tone of voice. Long, dark eyelashes fluttered in fascination for a moment, then she went back to her pebble.

Madison closed her eyes. "My dear ancestor Miss Cassie, I call out to you in gratitude and love. I want you to meet your descendent, Ivy Colleen. Yes, her first name is your friend's and her middle name is yours." She pointed at Ivy and kissed the crown of her head. Ivy shook her head and babbled, unwilling to give up on her new chew toy. "She was born the day before Christmas, the best present anyone could ever get.

"It's been a while since I've been here, what with winter socking us in and all. And I was pretty busy having this baby." She grinned and stroked her child's cheek, which garnered a huff at the disturbance while Ivy gnawed on her prize possession. "But it's early summertime now," Madison continued, "and the lilacs are in bloom. I hope you can smell them. The scent is intoxicating. I also hope you know how much I love you. You've inspired me more than you could ever know.

"For one thing, I finished high school in one semester. Yup. Just graduated with honors. And this fall I have a job as an aide at the clinic. I'm not old enough yet for EMT training but as soon as I am, I'll start that.

"And, Cassie, I have a best friend. A young man. I know people think I'm too young, but I think I'm falling in love with Eddie and he's falling in love with me. I know you married young, and I know it's possible to find love early in life, like you did. But I'm not in any rush. Best of all, though, is how much he adores Ivy. I could never love a man who didn't love my child.

"I feel you within my heart and soul, Cassie. I feel your strength. When I don't, whenever I feel weak, I remind myself of all that my ancestors went through to get me here. That always calms me down. They survived. You survived. I will, too.

"Well, that's it for now. I'll be back more often from now on. 'Bye for today."

Madison worked her way up to standing, taking Ivy with her. The child dropped her pebble in the process, yelped, and punched and kicked in distress. But suddenly she settled down, looked around with eyes as round as ripe blueberries, and gurgled with glee. Her pumping and bouncing became a merry dance in her mother's arms as she seemed to be celebrating some sacred event. Then, as if holding a conversation with an angel, she jabbered, halted as if listening, then jabbered some more, a radiant smile erupting across her rosy face. She made a final declaration, drooled again, and laughed heartily. Then she looked back at her mom as if saying, "Okay, I've said good-bye. We can go now."

The mom wiped her baby's mouth with the towel, went out around the fence, and strapped the infant into the carrier. She bent down and expertly hoisted it onto her back. As she rode her bike to the cottage with a full heart, knowing that not only were she and her child well loved by those here on this earth, they were loved by those in the Great Beyond, as well.

The End

THANK you for reading *The Promise of Christmas Present: A Mackinac Island Novella*. I hope it swept you away to the island as it did me while I was writing it. Here's a quick and easy link to its Amazon review, which is greatly appreciated:

https://amazon.com/review/create-review?&asin=B0C771ZHTQ

If you'd like to sign up for my twice-a-month newsletter for a free eBook, updates, and special offers, you'll find that on my website:

www.lindahughes.com

Free *Bonus Materials* – including the research links, resource books, websites, blogs, recipes, movies, playlist, extras, and more – used in writing my *Promise of Christmas* stories are waiting for you here:

https://dl.bookfunnel.com/taqatjwaoy

The third book in this Timeless Traditions Trilogy will be available in June, 2024. *The Promise of Christmas Future: A Mackinac Island Novella.*

ACKNOWLEDGMENTS

The Island Bookstore on Mackinac Island has been so very supportive of my books. I'm grateful to everyone there, including Mary Jane, Tamara, Jill, Emma, Jeremy, and anyone else there who has recommended my stories to readers. They always make book signings at their store easy and fun.

A big thank you also goes to the Addicted to Mackinac Island Facebook group for allowing me to post my new releases. Island lovers are so generous and kind in sharing my books with their own friends and followers.

And a hearty thanks to you, my readers, who make all this worthwhile. Without you, I would still write these stories because they come from my heart. But with you, they become a forum for us to connect over our love of Mackinac Island, Christmas stories, and family sagas. I am so grateful you are here to share that with me.

ABOUT THE AUTHOR

Award-winning author Linda Hughes writes romantic women's fiction and has twenty-five novels in publication. Her first visit to Mackinac Island was when she was nine. She's returned many times over the years.

You can learn more about Linda on her website at:
www.lindahughes.com